IN A
TREACHEROUS
COURT

IN A
TREACHEROUS
COURT

a novel

MICHELLE DIENER

GALLERY BOOKS

NEW YORK   LONDON   TORONTO   SYDNEY

Gallery Books
A Division of Simon & Schuster, Inc.
1230 Avenue of the Americas
New York, NY 10020

First Gallery Books trade paperback edition August 2011

GALLERY BOOKS and colophon are trademarks of Simon & Schuster, Inc.

For information about special discounts for bulk purchases, please contact Simon & Schuster Special Sales at 1-866-506-1949 or business@simonandschuster.com.

The Simon & Schuster Speakers Bureau can bring authors to your live event. For more information or to book an event, contact the Simon & Schuster Speakers Bureau at 1-866-248-3049 or visit our website at www.simonspeakers.com.

Designed by Jaime Putorti

Manufactured in the United States of America

10 9 8 7 6 5 4 3 2

Library of Congress Cataloging-in-Publication Data

Diener, Michelle.
    In a Treacherous Court / Michelle Diener.—1st Gallery Books trade paperback ed.
        p. cm.
    1. Henry VIII, King of England, 1491–1547—Fiction. 2. Courts and courtiers—Fiction. 3. Great Britain—History—Henry VIII, 1509–1547—Fiction. I. Title.
PR9619.4.D54I45 2011
823'.92—dc22
                2010045543

ISBN 978-1-4391-9708-0
ISBN 978-1-4391-9710-3 (ebook)

ACKNOWLEDGMENTS

This is my first published work and there have been many, many people along the way who have contributed to this moment. I offer apologies in advance for anyone I may forget.

First, I wish to thank my editor, Micki Nuding; her editorial assistant, Danielle Poiesz; and the rest of the team at Gallery Books, as well as my amazing agent, Marlene Stringer, for their enthusiasm and belief in this book. Thanks to them, this was all possible.

My critique partners, Edie Ramer and Liz Kreger, encouraged me, supported me, and told me when things needed to be cut or changed and when things were wonderful. I can only say thank you, although it doesn't seem enough.

My sister, Jo, has been my avid beta reader for years, and her enthusiasm and suggestions helped make this book better. Thank you.

From my original writing group, Allison Brennan, Karin Tabke, Maya Banks, Amy Knupp, Janette Kenny, and La-Donna Paulette gave me advice, help, and encouragement back when I was just starting to write seriously. Thank you for all your support.

I would also like to thank Julia Dekenah, Inge Tessendorf, Bridget Ryan, Frieda Lloyd, Amanda Wilson, Tabitha Yngstrom, Anna Suggitt, Kim Foster, and Fiona Cadogan for their support, enthusiasm, and encouragement of my writing journey. You are all good friends who lent me an ear when I needed it.

Thanks also to my book groups in Vredendal, Cape Town, and Australia. You were always supportive and encouraging. Thank you.

Thanks also to Mom, Dean, Lorna, Grant, and Shannon for their love and support of my dreams and goals through the years.

There have been many other people who have helped me on my journey, from my writing associations and from other walks of life. I can't mention you all, but thank you.

To my husband, who supported me and never once thought I wouldn't achieve my dreams, and to my children, who have learned to repeat themselves with good grace when their mother is so deep in her work she doesn't hear them the first time.

IN A
TREACHEROUS
COURT

1

The Chiefe Conditions and Qualities in a Courtier: To
be well borne and of a good stocke.

*Of the Chief Conditions and Qualityes in a Waytyng
Gentylwoman:* To be well born and of a good house.

—*The Courtyer of Count Baldessar Castilio divided into foure
bookes. Very necessary and profitatable for yonge Gentilmen
and Gentilwomen abiding in Court, Palaice or Place, done into
Englyshe by Thomas Hoby.*

FEBRUARY 1525

"I am the Keeper of Paradise, Purgatory, and Hell." John
Parker spoke through gritted teeth.

The shipping clerk who'd questioned his right to be on the
quay backed away, stammering, and Parker got a grip on his
annoyance. He wasn't used to being challenged these days.
He'd forgotten it brought out his temper.

His anger would have been hotter had the clerk let him
through unquestioned, though. The King's goods needed
ample protection.

The clerk sidled off and disappeared into the thick mist.

Still irritated, Parker scuffed his boot against a wharf pole and reflected that no good deed went unpunished.

The fog pressed all around, obscuring the merchants waiting along with him for the ship from the Netherlands. Their voices rose and fell in the swirling white, in tandem with the waves against the pier.

This was what arse-licking brought you: a fog-shrouded evening freezing your balls off, waiting to meet some nancy painter who would probably smell of garlic and pick his nose all the way back to London.

He thought of the Italian crossbows he'd taken delivery of earlier, the real reason for his business here, and felt an almost physical pang at being unable to unpack the beauties tonight.

The tread of a heavy boot thudded close by, muffled in the thick fog, and Parker turned toward it, his hand going under his cloak to his sword. He kept silent, listening intently when the footsteps stopped. His senses sharpened, honed from years of watching his own and the King's back, and he crept forward, soundless as the swirling fog.

A face loomed out of the white and Parker closed the distance, the rush of adrenaline in his blood.

"Ahhh." The man started back in terror, his cry of fear harsh and loud. His empty hands rose in surrender, and Parker relaxed, sliding the sword he didn't remember drawing back into its scabbard.

"Yes?"

It was another clerk, a black-robed, poxy-looking fellow. He rubbed shaking hands against his cloak. "Are you the King's man?"

"Aye." He was the King's man, all right. God help him.

"I have news of the ship from the Netherlands." The shipping clerk paused a moment, and to speed him up, Parker began drawing his sword again. "It put in northeast of here, at Deal," the man gasped. "There has been some trouble."

"What kind of trouble?"

The clerk shrugged. "Don't know."

Parker supposed he should be grateful the captain had the sense to keep whatever trouble plagued the King's ship away from the prying eyes and gossiping tongues here at Dover.

He faced northward and caught a glimpse of a lantern farther along the shore, a weak beacon in the bitter-cold dusk. He reached deep within for the strength to care enough to do the King's business.

"I'll fetch my horse."

———————

Susanna sat in the captain's cabin, a mug of wine cradled in her hands, staring into the dark red liquid as if it somehow held the answers.

Illogical though it might be, she could not bring herself to put the cup to her lips after seeing Master Harvey cough up so much blood. With a shudder, she put the cup on the table and pushed it away.

"Aye, it takes you like that sometimes." Dr. Pettigrew rose from his bench and went to stand beside the tiny window facing the docks. "Less and less as the years get on, though."

He spoke in French for her benefit, although her English was fluent enough, and Susanna thought he sounded sad. But a doctor must get used to death, surely?

"Here comes the King's man," he murmured, leaning closer to the thick, distorted circle of glass and looking out into the dark of early evening.

As he stepped back from the window, Susanna caught a flash of movement outside, the wave of a lantern, and heard the tread of authority on the gangplank.

"Thank God," she said. Pettigrew only lifted a white, bushy brow, as if he was not so sure they should be relieved.

Susanna stood. She felt too vulnerable in the low chair, and she and Pettigrew both faced the door as it opened.

The captain entered first, his face flushed by the warmth of the room after the freezing deck. Behind him came a man who was forced to duck to get through the door.

He had the hard look of a Swiss mercenary about him. His eyes were watchful, and the angles of his face showed no signs of easy living and indulgence, despite his fine clothes.

His brows were dark wings above his light eyes—gray or blue, she couldn't tell in the dim light of the cabin, but his black hair made them seem almost luminous.

He was a devil and an angel in one, and her fingers itched to paint him.

A long moment of silence filled the room as he studied her with the same intensity.

The captain coughed. "Mistress Horenbout, this is Master Parker, the King's Keeper of the Palace of Westminster and his Yeoman of the Crossbows. He was to meet you tonight and escort you to London. Now, of course, he will stay and attend to the . . . er . . . matter of Master Harvey."

"And a thorny matter it is," muttered Pettigrew, and Susanna saw the King's man start at his words, as if he'd only just realized the doctor was in the cabin with her. He was used to noticing everything, she thought, and she'd distracted him from that. Under normal circumstances, she would be flattered. But the circumstances tonight were anything but normal.

A man lay dead. Had died in her arms.

"Master Parker." She acknowledged him with a quick curtsy.

"Mistress Horenbout, if it pleases you, I will make arrangements for you to go ahead without me while I see to things here."

Her lips tightened at the trace of condescension in his tone. "As you wish, sir." She would be only too happy to get off this ship and into a warm bed.

"I will need to speak to all those who had dealings with Harvey while he was aboard, Captain." Parker's eyes rested thoughtfully on the doctor as Pettigrew lifted a mug of wine to his lips.

"That is what I thought," Captain Caitlin said. "That is why I bade them wait here for you."

Susanna watched Parker struggle to find the right meaning in the captain's words.

"Do I take it the only people Harvey spoke with while on board are these two?"

"In fact, Doctor Pettigrew only dealt with Master Harvey once he'd started coughing up his own lungs," Susanna said, repressing the tremble in her voice. "The only person he spoke with, or had anything to do with while on board, was me."

She was trouble. He'd heard of these women in the Netherlands and Italy, whose fathers took them into their studios and trained them in the arts of painting and sculpture along with their brothers, but he'd never met one. It looked like he'd caught himself a fine specimen now.

She sat opposite him, alone in the captain's cabin, and the light gleamed like fine brandy off her hair. Her face was the shape of a heart, but it was her eyes that drew him. An intriguing mix of green and hazel, they were never still, taking in everything around her. She would make a good spy.

Perhaps she was one.

Harvey certainly had been, and after closeting himself in her company aboard the ship, he had died.

Parker was no spymaster, but he was close enough to the right circles to know Harvey never came back from the Netherlands without information. Chances were he'd had something interesting to impart this time as well.

"Will you be the one to tell his wife he is dead?" she asked, breaking the silence.

"Perhaps. I'm not sure." He leaned forward. "How do you know he was married?"

"He told me. Gave me a message for his wife if he did not make it alive across the Channel. And the few other times we met, he'd spoken of her."

Parker's eyes narrowed. *She knew him before?* He kept his voice steady. "He thought he might not make it across?"

She shook her head, blinking her eyes. Her teeth bit down on her full bottom lip. "He only just made it on board. He leaped on as the ship pulled away. The men chasing him could do nothing but watch as we sailed off." Her eyes glittered with unspilled tears. "He gave them a most jaunty wave when we were safely out of their reach, but it was all bravado. One of them had managed to get a knife in his lung before he escaped them."

"Did you see who was chasing him?"

Susanna nodded. "I saw them, but I didn't know them. They were strangers to me."

Parker let that pass. "You say you've met Harvey before?"

"A few times, at the palace." Mistress Horenbout scrubbed at her eyes. "He was a cloth merchant and had business with Margaret of Austria. My father and I met him on occasion while we all waited our turn to speak with her."

"Your father was commissioned by Her Highness?"

She nodded. "My father has been her painter for many years."

He could hear the pride in her voice.

Time to get back to the business at hand. "What did Harvey tell you before he died?"

"I'm afraid I cannot tell you, sir."

Parker blinked. "Cannot?" Did she mean Harvey had been unintelligible?

Susanna nodded, her face solemn. "He made me swear I would tell no one but King Henry himself."

Parker's lips thinned. "I am the King's trusted yeoman. I will make sure the message reaches him."

She shook her head. "I gave my word to a dying man. Besides, I am here at the King's invitation. I expect to be received by him. I can tell him myself easily enough."

She was uncomfortable defying him, he could see, but the set of her mouth was stubborn.

"The message may be urgent." He struggled to keep his voice cool, neither pleading nor bullying. Simply stating a fact.

"Perhaps. But could you, in truth, give it to the King much before I?"

"I could ride with it tonight."

She shook her head again and stood with the fluid grace of a swan. He pushed himself out of his own chair and towered over her. Crowded her.

"You should tell me."

She drew in a deep breath and threw back her shoulders. "I will not be forced to act dishonorably."

He stared at her and the silence stretched out.

She shot him a cool look and made for the door, her shoulder brushing against him. As her hair passed under his nose, he smelled rosemary. He breathed it deep into his lungs. Despite her refusal to accede to him, he couldn't help the smile that broke across his face.

She most definitely did not smell of garlic, and he was sure picking her nose was the last thing on her mind.

He had just decided arse-licking *did* sometimes work out to be advantageous, when a crossbow bolt shattered the cabin's window and buried itself deep in the oak door, just a whisker above Susanna Horenbout's left shoulder.

Parker threw himself toward the window. Unless there was more than one of them, he had a few moments before the shooter could load the next bolt. But the shatter of glass had aroused attention, and some of the crew rushed down the gangplank, shouting.

Parker saw the billow of a cape as a dark figure ducked behind a warehouse, and knew the shooter was gone.

He turned back to the artist, who stood frozen, her gaze fixed on the door. The bolt still vibrated where it was embedded in the wood, and when she turned to look at him over her shoulder, her eyes were wide with shock.

"It seems someone wants Harvey's secret to die with you, madam."

His words made her shudder.

She regarded him with eyes as fathomless as the sea. "Then you'll have to make sure they don't succeed."

2

The Chiefe Conditions and Qualities in a Courtier: To
play well at fense upon all kinde of weapons.

*Of the Chief Conditions and Qualityes in a Waytyng
Gentylwoman:* To accompany sober and quiet
maners and honesty with a livelie quicknesse of wit.

He'd thought she would fuss at having a man in her
chamber, but Susanna Horenbout only had eyes for the
large feather bed in the center of the room and the steaming
bath that sat behind a cheap wooden screen.

She staggered toward the bath and was already loosening
the ties at the back of her dress before she disappeared from
view.

Parker turned toward the door, and though he had checked
the lock, checked it again.

He heard her sink down into the water, groaning as if relieved
of an infinite burden, and again felt a smile tug at his mouth.

That she could raise his spirits even in their current circumstances disturbed him.

He lifted the heavy, elaborate gold collar over his head, a literal reminder of the weight of his office, and unclasped his fine wool cloak, hanging both over a chair near the fire. Then he sat down and pulled off his boots, neatly standing them beneath the chair before tugging at the laces of his doublet.

He knew the King's intimates would sneer at the careful way he treated his clothes, but the memory of a hungry belly and a thin cloak were too fresh in his mind.

He took nothing for granted.

Perhaps that was why the King trusted him.

He heard Susanna rise from the bath with a cascade of water, and dry herself, then saw the tips of her fingers above the screen as she pulled her shift over her head.

She looked hollow-eyed when she stepped into view. She didn't speak, just staggered to the bed and crawled beneath the covers.

She murmured something as her eyes closed.

"Pardon?" Parker took a step toward her, leaning down to hear her better.

"Thank you," she muttered, her voice a hoarse whisper, and then, curled up like a babe, she fell asleep.

Parker eyed the bed he'd been looking forward to since waiting on the docks for her with regret. Only one small corner of it was occupied by Susanna Horenbout, but she might as well have been spread-eagled across it.

He took the pallet the surprised innkeeper had provided and tossed it down before the door.

This wasn't the first time he'd guarded a doorway, and

since someone thought Susanna's secret was worth killing for, it was unlikely to be the last.

Somehow, as he heard a faint sigh come from the bed, that thought was not as irritating as it should have been.

———————

Susanna woke with the uncomfortable feeling of being watched. She snapped open her eyes and was ensnared in the silver-blue of her guardian devil's gaze.

"You have good instincts," he said.

She shrugged and snuggled deeper into the covers. She could say she was an artist, sensitive to atmosphere, but in truth, at home she was watched all the time, and her instincts were finely honed.

He was as disheveled as she must be, blue-black stubble darkening his jaw, his unfashionably short hair standing every which way. He wore only his fine linen shirt, the drawstring loose at the neck, and his breeches.

His feet were bare, and unable to help herself, she leaned over the edge of the bed and stared down at them.

He wiggled his toes. "Never seen a man's feet before?"

She ignored him, not caring about propriety. His feet were magnificent. She must . . .

She struggled up, swung down her legs, and reached under the bed for her satchel, wincing as her feet met the cold stone floor. She quickly pulled them back up and took paper and a piece of charcoal, as well as her pressing board, from the bag.

"What are you doing?" Parker asked, bemused and suspicious.

"Shh."

She hated people talking to her while she worked. She needed a quiet, focused mind.

She began to draw, her first strokes, as always, a sensual delight, full of possibilities. She made them with a flourish, then settled down to the real work. Parker began to move away and she gave a shout, her left hand shooting out to grab his shirt and keep him in place while her right carried on, the charcoal vibrating and twisting between her fingers with a life of its own.

"This floor is freezing, mistress, and if you think I'm going to stand here while you draw my *feet* . . ."

She let go of his shirt and leaned back, studying the results with the hypercritical eye her father had coached her to use. She'd drawn just his toes and about half of his foot.

She gave a nod. It wasn't bad.

She felt the paper being pried from her fingers, and resisted in surprise for a moment before letting go. She saw Parker's eyes widen, and then his startled expression as he jerked his gaze from the drawing to her face.

"That took you less than five minutes."

"It's just a simple sketch."

But it wasn't, and she knew it. When she *had* to draw, no matter the situation, no matter the time, then the result was very seldom a simple sketch.

Albrecht Dürer himself had bought a *plätlein* of the Savior from her, exclaiming that he never thought a girl could accomplish so much.

The sting of that backhanded compliment was less, coming as it did from one of the world's finest artists. Also because he'd thought her work good enough to pay money for. There was no greater artistic compliment than that.

"You really can draw."

Parker looked so astonished, she laughed.

"My father would not have sent me to represent his atelier unless I was the very best he had available."

His eyes narrowed. "He is taking a risk, though. Sending you." He looked her up and down, and there was no mistaking he liked what he saw. "England is not used to women artists, and a beautiful woman on her own anywhere is unsafe, no matter what her skills."

"All things my father considered and agonized over, I can assure you."

Parker raised an eyebrow. "Then why?"

Susanna looked at him for a long moment, at the way his thick, dark lashes framed his eyes, the hardness and the pureness shining out of him. She swallowed. "It was a case of better the devil he didn't know. If I had stayed in Ghent, my father knew it was only a matter of time before I seduced his blacksmith."

Susanna Horenbout knew how to surprise a man. Parker studied her profile as she sat primly on the cart his horse kept pace with.

She was exotic in every way—from her accent, to the cut of her dress and the hood that framed hair like honeyed wine, to the way she could craft a masterpiece in a moment, of his *feet*, no less.

Parker had never met her like before.

And a bolt aimed at her back had nearly met its mark yesterday.

Parker concentrated again on the road ahead, on identifying the places most likely to be used for ambush. They were exposed, riding with only the King's colors and Parker's sword for protection—more than enough, under normal circumstances, but nothing about this was normal.

He could have waited to send word for guards from London, but in the time it would take for the message to reach court, and the men he needed dispatched, they could have ridden to London and back twice.

With any luck, they had left the assassin from last night behind them. It would be courting danger to remain in either Deal or Dover.

Parker felt a quick, hot anger for Harvey, the man who had died in Susanna's arms. He hadn't known the man well, but Harvey had had no need to spy for the King. He was a genuine merchant conducting a profitable business with the Netherlands and France.

Had Harvey realized how deep a game he'd been playing? Or was there some other reason he would risk his life to pass on information?

He wanted to ask Susanna again if she would tell him Harvey's secret. But Simon, the cart driver who'd accompanied him to the docks, sat right beside her, tight-faced with the effort of forcing his team to do double time over bad roads pitted by the rains.

At least it wasn't raining now, although the heavy, dark skies promised to change that at any moment.

Parker glanced at the back of the cart to make sure the canvas protecting his Italian crossbows was in place. The inlay in their gleaming wood stocks was a thing of beauty, and he wanted them in perfect condition when they reached the King.

A short distance ahead the road disappeared into a thick wood, and Parker surged forward, giving Gawain his head.

"Problem?" Simon called.

"Just making sure," Parker called back, flicking his cloak back from his scabbard for easy access to his sword.

As he thundered toward the wood, it was Gawain who saved him.

The massive charger gave a little jump that braked their advance. They skidded through the wet leaves just as they came under the first trees, and the arrow missed Parker by a hair.

He felt the brush of the feathered end on his cheek as it shot past, and an involuntary shout tore from his throat.

He hauled Gawain up on his back legs, forelegs windmilling, and urged him around as fast as he could. Two arrows flew just above him.

"Attack!" As he charged back along the path he saw Simon turn the cart sharp left off the road, urging the horses over the stony ground.

Simon suddenly hauled back on the reins, and Parker saw another archer rise from behind a large bush in front of the cart, his arrow lit.

Parker swore, and dug desperate heels into Gawain's sides, racing back to the cart as Simon fought to bring it to a halt.

The archer in the field took deliberate aim at the horses. The burning arrow arched between them and they went wild, leaping to the side with screams of fear. The cart slid on the mud-slicked ground, pivoted so it stood at an angle to the woods.

Simon scrambled down to uncouple the horses before they broke a leg or pulled the cart over, and Parker reached them just as Susanna took cover behind the cart. He leaped down from Gawain and slapped his hindquarters to keep the stallion going, following the cart horses into the open field next to the wood.

"How many?" Simon threw himself on the ground beside Parker, and Parker's estimation of him soared even higher. The cartman was on edge but cool, his voice and his hands steady.

"Not sure. At least two longbows in the woods besides the one in the field." Quiet had descended for a moment, and Parker watched the woods from under the cart.

Simon touched his arm and held up a knife with a sharp blade and a battered hilt, then jerked his head in the direction of the trees.

"You want to attack longbowmen with a knife across open ground?" Parker shook his head in disbelief as a fresh volley of arrows struck the cart.

"We must do something." Susanna Horenbout's voice was as steady as Simon's as she wriggled beneath the cart beside him.

Parker felt the heat of her pressed against his side. "We have but two knives and a sword. Unless you have any weapons hidden beneath your gown?"

"Is a crossbow easy to use?" Susanna asked.

"That is the beauty of them. Anyone can learn to use a crossbow. The drawback is in the time it takes to reload. A longbowman can loose two arrows to every bolt." Parker kept his focus on the trees. "It doesn't shoot as far as a longbow, either, but you can load it ahead of time, then shoot when you need to."

"So"—as Susanna spoke, two more arrows arced from the trees and thumped into the cart—"if you had a great many crossbows, you could load them in advance? Lie under this cart and shoot them off one by one?"

"You could indeed." Parker had never felt more stupid in his life. Even now, he almost balked at using the beauties. They were the property of the King—but what was this but the King's business?

"What?" Simon frowned at him.

Parker's voice was dry. "Mistress Horenbout has quite correctly reminded me that we have thirty Italian crossbows in the cart above us, with bolts."

Simon let out a whoop of laughter, and thumped the ground with his fist.

3

The Chiefe Conditions and Qualities in a Courtier:
Not to hasarde himself in forraginge and spoiling or
in enterprises of great daunger and small estimation,
though he be sure to gaine by it.

*Of the Chief Conditions and Qualityes in a Waytyng
Gentylwoman:* To be good and discreete.

The archer in the field fired his second burning arrow,
aiming it low. Susanna fumbled the bolt in her hands as
she looked back and saw smoke rising from its burning tip, fifty
feet behind them in the long grass.

When she turned back, the other archers were stepping
out of the woods, and she saw with a leap of panic that their
arrows were lit as well. They intended to burn the cart and
those under it, or shoot them as they tried to run to safety.

She caught hold of herself, rammed the bolt into place,
and turned the cranequin as hard as she could.

Parker lay still beside her, his shoulders and arms bunched,
his eyes intent on his prey. Susanna was fascinated by his
finger, the way it caressed the trigger; with a minute, incre-

mental tightening until, with a rush of air and a recoil that made her jerk, he loosed his bolt.

The archer on the right fell screaming to the ground, the bolt in his shoulder. He began crawling like a pitiful caterpillar back toward the cover of the woods.

The other man turned tail and ran after him, loosing his burning arrow, which landed in an uncooperative, wet field to the left of the cart.

He stumbled just before the trees, and Susanna saw the bloom of blood on his dark green doublet as he fell face-first into the loamy soil at the edge of the wood.

"Could there be more of them?" Simon asked, his crossbow held loosely in his grip, and she realized the third archer was down.

Parker grunted, noncommittal, but Susanna noticed his hands were relaxed on his bow.

Rather than look at the fallen men while they waited to be sure, she watched the misfired arrow burn down its length. It petered out in a desultory trail of smoke, leaving an unpleasant smell of burned tar and feathers drifting in the air.

She didn't want to look at the bodies.

Her passage from Ghent was marked by a trail of blood.

"There is no one else. Or they have made off." Parker stood, still keeping the cart between himself and the woods. Only when the birds began calling in the trees again did he move around it.

"Get the horses," he told Simon. Then he walked, unhurried, toward the men he'd brought down.

Simon watched him a moment, then walked away to the field where the horses stood grazing and whistled to them.

Parker was crouched beside the first man he'd hit. Steeling herself, Susanna walked across the field to join them.

"Who sent you?" Parker loomed over the archer.

"I do not know who . . ." The man choked, then turned his head to retch in the grass.

"Of course you do," Parker said, his tone friendly. He reached forward and grasped the end of the bolt that protruded from the man's shoulder, gave it a small twist.

The archer's shriek cut through the air, causing crows to lift from the trees squawking, and Susanna's heart to stop.

"No." The man's voice was a quiet sob when he could speak again. "No."

"Yes and yes." Parker reached out again, and it was on Susanna's lips to scream "No!," to leap forward and stay his hand.

"One thing! I know one thing." The archer shivered uncontrollably.

Parker said nothing, his fingers a mere whisper from the bolt.

"His face was . . . cloaked. But his hands. Saw his hands as he gave over the coin." The archer's breath was labored and he closed his eyes a moment.

Parker's fingers twitched.

"They were the hands of an old man. Not a laborer—they weren't callused." The archer choked again. "That is all I know."

Parker leaned in closer. "How were you to let him know the job was done?"

The archer coughed, a rattling sound that made Susanna's stomach heave. "Said . . . his master would know. When you did or did not return to court."

Parker stood, impatience in every line of him, his eyes on Simon hooking the horses back into their harness.

Susanna stepped away from the archer, unsure what to do. Her gaze fell on the body of the other man and she jerked it away, shivering. He lay with his face in the wet earth, his hand outstretched, his bow flung from him.

Parker bent and gathered up the archer's bow and arrows, and raised an eyebrow at Susanna's gasp of shock.

"You'd rather I leave them here for some brigand to take and use against the innocent?" He stepped away, and gathered the bows of the other two men.

Susanna shook her head. She hadn't thought of that. "What will we do about him?" She gestured to the wounded archer. He lay still, eyes closed.

Parker looked across at him, then walked back toward the cart, and Susanna trailed him reluctantly.

"Sir! What will we do?"

"He tried to kill us. Why should we do anything?"

Susanna stopped and half-turned back to where the man lay. She bit her lip as one of the crows hopped toward him, almost close enough to peck. She wrung her hands and met Parker's steady gaze.

"Please. Let us take him in the cart."

"We could repack the crossbows," Simon said from behind Parker. "Make room for him in the back."

Parker turned to look at his driver, and Susanna could see veiled amusement in Simon's expression.

"Very well." He flicked back the canvas, and his hand rested reverently on the polished crossbows beneath it. "If only because it will be interesting to see who at court tries to kill him when they realize who he is."

———

London was a cesspit of mud and filth.

The hard rain stabbed cold needles into her shoulders and head, and a sour, putrid smell reached out at them from every alley they passed.

"Not long now," Simon told her, and Susanna nodded, hunching as deep into her cloak as she could. Not that it made a difference; she was wet through.

She had never felt so strange. Out of sorts, exhausted, and distant from herself. The comforts and routine of Ghent were far behind.

She looked across at Parker, who must be exhausted himself—he'd been tense and alert since the attack yesterday morning. He hadn't relaxed his posture for a moment, not even last night in the inn where they had snatched a few hours of sleep.

Now that they were in London, he was stiffer still.

Somewhere in the King's palace sat a spider in his web, watching and waiting to see if his prey had escaped his trap.

Susanna wondered what Parker was going to do about that, but she was too miserable and cold to think it through herself.

She was on foreign soil, and he would know far better than she the best way to flush out a traitor.

Part of his plan lay shivering under the canvas at the back of the cart. Parker had insisted they not pull the bolt out of the archer's shoulder until they had a physician to hand; the man would bleed to death otherwise. And he wanted to keep the man alive so he could watch who sought him out at court. Or tried to kill him.

Susanna shivered. She was an artist; she knew nothing of this kind of intrigue. Killing assassins. Finding traitors. Exposing spies.

She would happily leave that to Parker.

"We're here." Simon managed to sound cheerful, as if they'd had a pleasant, uneventful journey in good weather, rather than the opposite.

Susanna bit her tongue against her sarcastic rejoinder. She knew from other Ghent artists that it didn't take much for the English to work up a grudge.

Some Englishmen felt threatened by the King's penchant for European artists.

Klaas Groenewalt, a tapestry cartoonist who worked with her father occasionally and who had tutored her in English since her father made the decision to send her to London, had warned her to watch her back and be polite at all times. The knife wound scar on his forearm proved he spoke from experience.

His tale had almost made her father change his mind. She'd seen the struggle on his face, and then his eye had fallen on Joost, shirtless and stoking the fire, and his expression had hardened again.

Susanna roused herself from her memories. It was time to take note of her surroundings. They were entering the gates of Bridewell Palace, and she would need all her wits about her.

4

The Chiefe Conditions and Qualities in a Courtier: To procure where ever he goeth that men may first conceive a good opinion of him before he commeth there.

Of the Chief Conditions and Qualityes in a Waytyng Gentylwoman: To take hede that give none occasion to bee yll reported of.

Susanna was the only woman.

Men stood or sat where they could in the antechamber in which Parker had left her, giving the impression of a flock of discontented crows in their black doublets and cloaks. Their thin black legs ended in wide-toed shoes that tapped impatiently as the minutes dragged by.

Parker had long since disappeared, and she had had ample time to sit and admire the workmanship in the flourishes of the room, the carvings and the furniture, the intricate silk paneling on the walls.

The guards at the entrance to the privy chamber had watched her with interest at first. Parker had murmured something in their ears before they'd let him into the King's innermost sanctum, and the curiosity in their eyes was blatant.

Susanna could only assume he'd told them to make sure no one tried to kill her. For the third time in three days.

But even potential murder victims lost their allure after time, and as others came and went, the guards' attention shifted.

Some of the courtiers looked at her with curiosity, others with hostility. A few murmured greetings to each other or struck up quiet conversations in the corners of the room, but it seemed their eyes always came back to rest on her.

Furtive glances whirled around the room, and Susanna needed something to absorb her attention so she wouldn't have to eye everyone back.

She was taken with the way the guards framed the door, the way they formed the focal point of the room. She took out a piece of paper and her charcoal and began to sketch.

Her training had been in illumination, and she saw each scene as a hundred small, intricate pictures, pieced together to form the whole. She did not balk at spending time on the pattern of the guards' doublets. On the texture of the wall behind them. On the shadow cast by their halberds.

But there was no fun for her in producing a faithful rendition of the scene. She slipped in a tiny mouse, peeping from behind a guard's shoe. A cat—plenty of those had slunk past her as she waited—crouched under a heavy chair, shoulders hunched, weight forward, its eyes steady in readiness to pounce.

From the patterned silk paneling, a small songbird broke

free of the fabric and fluttered up to perch on a wooden window frame.

She shaded the frown on one of the clerics waiting with her, considered giving him just the merest hint of devil's horns peeping up from his straight brown hair.

"Mistress Horenbout."

Parker's voice jerked her back to the reality she was subverting.

He was before her, his boots almost touching hers, and she hadn't noticed him.

"I see you've kept yourself busy." His eyes were on the sketch, and he reached out a finger and touched a corner of the paper reverently. "The King will like this."

"Then he shall have it." Susanna regretted her offer the moment it was made. This had been done for her own amusement.

"I'm afraid the wait will be longer still. It is time for the King's repast, but he shall see you directly after. I would have you wait in his privy chamber, though."

Parker's eyes did a quick scan of the room, and Susanna realized he'd been worried about her, hadn't liked leaving her alone so long.

She stared up at him. If the courtiers waiting here were crows, he was a bird of prey. His power and strength caused a skip in her chest.

He bent down to her, and the atmosphere in the chamber finally penetrated her self-induced fog. Avid curiosity. And not a small helping of resentment.

"I am in no danger. The guards are nearby." She spoke for his ear alone, her lips almost brushing his skin as she allowed him to take her hand and help her up.

"So is the man who paid those archers," Parker reminded her, equally quiet. He did not move back to give her space as she stood, and his body brushed hers as he picked up her satchel. He hefted the weight of it with surprise.

"Come." He turned back to the door, waiting for her to precede him past the guards, who had opened the door just enough to let them through.

One of the courtiers, who had been waiting at least as long as she, hissed in fury as they stepped across the threshold.

Susanna felt a skip of excitement and nerves in the pit of her stomach. She was about to come face to face with the King of England.

S he and Parker had waited for the King through thirteen dishes, each one served with the ceremony of a state occasion, but the meal was at last at an end.

The King rose from the elevated, canopied table set for one, and the conversations of the courtiers who stood on either side and behind him quieted. Susanna was struck by the tableau they made, the dark colors of their robes strangely lit by the rain-muted light from the tall windows. The King, by contrast, shone brighter than a freshly drawn illumination in his scarlet and gold.

Susanna looked down at the charcoal drawing of the scene she'd made to spin out the time, and wished for her paints.

Henry looked directly at Parker and nodded, then turned and walked through the courtiers to the door leading to his privy lodgings. Moses could not have parted the Red Sea more efficiently than the King parted the crowd as he made his way across the room.

Parker stood, his frown lifting, and Susanna rose with him. He took her elbow and made to follow in the King's wake.

But the Red Sea was merging again, determined to see nothing special about Moses' followers. A wave of bodies surged back into place, set on being merry, loud, and unseeing.

Susanna looked up at Parker, and was surprised to see his mouth twitch in amusement.

He steered her around the crush, keeping close to the wall, and they made their way to the door without much more jostling.

"You're a popular man," Susanna murmured.

Parker smiled. "I gauge my popularity by the number of snubs I receive. The more, the better."

Susanna flashed him a look, saw his cheerfulness was genuine.

Once more, the door was guarded by two men. As they moved aside to let them through, both regarded Parker with respect. Unlike the courtiers, these men were Parker's allies.

They stepped into a short passage and turned into the smaller room of the King's closet, and Susanna was surprised to see that no one else was present. Just the two of them and the English King, in a room with a large desk and tables covered in maps and books.

She felt the clench of nerves, and curtsied long and low, her eyes on the Turkish carpet.

Acknowledging her tribute with a nod and a gleam of curiosity, the King clapped a hand on Parker's shoulder. "I hear you had cause to test my new bows?"

Parker smiled for the first time since they'd entered the palace, and relaxed. "Aye. Didn't think I'd have to use them in earnest quite so soon."

"How did they perform?"

"I only loosed two bolts. Both hit their mark." Parker's voice was filled with satisfaction.

Henry laughed, and she was struck by how handsome he was, with his red-gold hair, his broad shoulders, his piercing blue eyes. He radiated charisma.

As if he'd read her thoughts, he sent her a smile full of charm, and she could not help the smile she sent back.

"I am as curious as a young boy to know whom Parker brings to me with whispers of secrets and ambushes and murder." Henry looked at the paper in her hand, and held out his own. "I saw you working on this in the privy chamber. May I?"

Susanna presented her sketch to him. She had restrained the temptation to fantasize. She'd known there was a chance it would end up in the King's hand, and she did not yet know what did and did not cause offense.

His eyes widened, just as Parker's had that first morning at the inn. He cast a glance across at Parker, as if to confirm this really was the work of a woman's hand. From long practice, Susanna suppressed her frustration and hurt. Her father had given her a mixed blessing when he'd taken her into his ate-lier: the chance to shine, and the burden of seeing men try to dull that shine at every turn.

Even so, she wouldn't change a single step that had led her to this moment.

"Your Majesty, I present to you your new painter from Ghent, Mistress Susanna Horenbout."

"Horenbout?" The King took a step back, his eyes going from the sketch to Susanna. "But I thought . . ."

"My father will send my brother, Lucas, as soon as he is re-turned from Nuremberg, Your Majesty. But I am as able as my brother in illumination and painting. My father would not have sent me otherwise."

Henry looked at the sketch again. He wanted to be gallant, she could see. If he was honest, he'd admit the evidence before him was proof of her claim. Yet she was a woman.

"Aye. You have talent." He regarded her for a long moment, and Susanna had to bow her head so as not to stare back. She knew her court etiquette.

"We have more pressing things to discuss." Parker broke the silence, his tone crisp. "Such as Master Harvey."

"Harvey?" Henry moved toward a small arrangement of chairs, and indicated that they take seats. "The merchant?"

"The recently murdered merchant," Parker told him as he waited for Susanna to sit before taking his own chair.

Henry glanced at Susanna, as if unsure whether they should be discussing the death of a spy in front of her, but Parker flicked his hand, cutting through the uncertainty.

"Mistress Horenbout witnessed Harvey's flight from a . . . group of brigands." Parker looked at her as he spoke, and something in his eyes started a faint buzz in her ears, a prickle along the tops of her arms. "Harvey was stabbed before he escaped them. Mistress Horenbout knew Harvey from her and her father's business at Margaret's court, and she cared for him while he lay dying."

Henry was taking in Parker's words, weighing the implications.

"Harvey had an important message, Your Majesty. One that he entrusted to Mistress Horenbout with his dying breath."

Henry sat forward, his interest sharp, his eyes on Parker's face. "What was it?"

"You will have to ask your painter, my lord. On her honor, she swore to tell you alone."

He no longer spoke about it with any heat, and Susanna raised her eyes to his. "My word is my bond."

She had the regent's full attention, now, and she forced her gaze back to her lap.

"Well, out with it, gal."

Susanna suddenly felt stricken. She had a feeling this message would not be well received.

She settled her gaze on the brooch at the King's throat. "Master Harvey bade me tell you he heard a whisper that the French King has signed a secret agreement with Pope Clement in the war against the Emperor. King Francis has promised Richard de la Pole he will use his new papal influence to strengthen de la Pole's claim to the throne of England. Harvey also heard that de la Pole has already begun feeling out who in England will support him if he receives his papal dispensation."

Susanna took a deep breath, and tried to block out the image of Harvey in his last moments. "He said he had discovered how de la Pole was sending messages into England."

The clock on Henry's desk ticked off the silence. Henry's eyes were intent on her face, and she shifted uncomfortably.

"How is de la Pole doing it?" Parker's question cut through the quiet.

Susanna shook her head. "Master Harvey never said. He was breathing his last. I think he only entrusted me with the message at all because he could see Death's shade hovering above him." She looked up to the ceiling and blinked, to keep the tears that had welled from falling. "He broke off what he was saying and looked past my shoulder, as if he truly could see Death standing behind me." Susanna shivered. "He whispered a last message for his wife, and then he retched up blood and died minutes later."

Again there was silence in the room.

"Does anyone else know what you have just told me?" Henry leaned forward, eyes frightening, as if he were on the edge of a terrible rage. The charming bonhomie was replaced with ruthlessness, cold as the blade of an executioner's axe.

Susanna shook her head, but it was Parker who spoke.

"Harvey died in Mistress Horenbout's arms, Your Majesty, and she confined herself to the captain's cabin thereafter to wait for me. An attempt was made on her life while we were still aboard the ship, and I have been constantly at her side ever since, as she would give her message only to you."

"As ever, you have done exceedingly well, Parker." As he addressed Parker, the King's ruthlessness gave way to affection and respect. But when he swung his gaze back to her, Susanna had to suppress a shiver. "And I owe my thanks to you, Mistress Horenbout, for your honorable conduct. Your discretion is to your credit. And I hope you will continue to exercise it."

It was a warning. And a threat.

Susanna dipped her head in acknowledgment.

"I will ensure that Mistress Horenbout comes to no further harm." Parker leaned toward Henry, his tone clear. He was saying: *I'll make sure she keeps quiet.*

Susanna watched him steadily, but his expression was neutral. He did that well, she realized.

"Good." Henry rose and walked across to the window, looked down into the courtyard beyond. "Keep her close, Parker. I can send what limning I would have her do through your office. And watch your own back."

"Is there anything else I can do for you regarding this matter?" Parker stood as well, and Susanna followed suit.

"No. I have ways of discovering who may be turning their loyalty from me to that Yorkist pretender dog, de la Pole. Ways that are much more subtle than you are used to, Parker."

Parker's mouth thinned into a tight line of anger. "Harvey was killed getting this message to you, Your Majesty. Some person has twice tried to kill Mistress Horenbout to prevent her from reaching you with his last words. The second time, he included me in his plans. I would like to find out who he is." He spoke plainly, with no attempt to soften what he said.

"You're too straight, Parker." Henry turned. "And why would he try again? Mistress Horenbout *has* reached me. The danger to her is surely over."

"That is not something I would wager upon." Parker's words were stark and hard, like the man himself, but the King took no umbrage. Instead, it seemed that he relaxed further, as if, in not even trying to curry favor, Parker was showing himself to be trustworthy.

"Then keep your sword arm strong and your blade in your boot." It was a dismissal.

Susanna curtsied. She murmured something by way of fare-well, and Parker took her arm and led her from the room.

She barely saw the guards at the door, and though she registered the courtiers watching them with the intensity of lap-dogs waiting for a tidbit, they were in her periphery. Spinning round and round in her head was the cold, terror-inducing fact that the King of England was afraid.

And she was the cause of it.

5

The Chiefe Conditions and Qualities in a Courtier:
Not to carie about tales and triflinge newis.

Of the Chief Conditions and Qualityes in a Waytyng Gentylwoman: To have an understandinge in all thinges belonginge to the Courtier, that she maye gyve her judgemente to commend and to make of gentilmen according to their worthinesse and desertes.

Parker watched Susanna from the doorway, watched the sensuous movement of her hands over the smooth stocks of his crossbows. "Beautiful, aren't they?"

She jumped and spun, her hand going to her throat. She did not scold him for startling her, but relaxed and turned back to the table. Her fingers again traced the patterns inlaid in the wood.

She had been waiting for him to conduct his business and enter the new crossbows into the register for a half hour, and it was bitterly cold in the unheated storeroom. Parker felt guilty for leaving her here, but at least she'd been safe under the protection of the yeomen guards.

"They are beautiful. A marriage of art and function. Does it take much time to master them?"

"Aye. Though it's easier than the longbow." Parker studied her as she turned to face him. "Do you have a mind to learn?"

"I do."

Parker shook his head, surprised to be taken up on his joke.

"You do not approve of women who seek to learn to protect themselves?"

"A bow is an attacking weapon or a siege weapon. It will do you no good on the streets of London." Parker flung a canvas sheet over the bows to shield them from dust.

"What is a good weapon on the streets of London, then?" Susanna seemed in earnest.

Parker hesitated, then dug into his boot and brought out a wicked-looking blade. "This, held ready in the palm of the hand, mostly covered by a sleeve."

The blood drained from her face. A knife was an up-close weapon. Personal. No nice distance, like a bow.

She shook her head. "Then I'll have to go about London unarmed."

"It matters not." Parker stepped forward and held out his hand to escort her from the munitions storehouse.

"Why?" She slipped her hand into his, and the way she did it, without hesitation, tightened something within him. The sharp flash of feeling made him suck in his breath.

"Because wherever you go in the streets of London, I will be just one step behind, mistress. And I have enough weapons for both of us."

Her fingers tightened around his hand. "Surely the danger

is past? The whole court must know we have seen the King, that I have conveyed whatever message I might carry."

Parker stood close to her, unwilling to leave the dark intimacy of the storeroom and go out into the busy, snow-dirtied courtyard beyond.

"Until we know your attacker's motives, I do not wish to take a chance."

"What will we do?" She seemed sure he would know.

"We hide you somewhere safe, and then I watch to see who tries to kill the archer."

"Where is he? Is he recovered?"

Parker shook his head. "The bolt has been removed. I had one of the King's own surgeons see to it. He is in the infirmary in Blackfriars Monastery, next to the palace. The monks think he will live—if his former patron does not silence him first."

Susanna lifted her head, her eyes suddenly wide. "You did not tell the King about the archer."

"No, I didn't."

She held his gaze in that forthright way of hers. "Why not?"

"Because no one tries to kill me without my taking a very personal interest in discovering who they are."

She watched him for a long moment. "What were you before you became the King's man, Master Parker?"

He felt himself sink into the green-brown of her eyes, calm and serene as a wood in spring. She could see straight to his soul. He did not know whether he should rejoice at that, or despair.

He led them through the door out into the freezing rain. "I was nothing."

————————

"Welcome to Paradise." Parker spoke with a lift in his voice, as if the words were a private joke.

Susanna looked up at the house before her. "Very nice." It was beautiful, but she couldn't find the energy for enthusiasm.

Dusk was already settling, and she had yet to find a hearth to warm her feet. Parker needed to fetch his things from his palace lodgings at Westminster before taking her to his own house, which she gathered he seldom used. All his clothes were here.

"This won't take long." Parker opened the door with a key he'd taken from his pouch, and gave a small bow and a flourish for her to precede him.

Grateful to be out of the rain, Susanna entered a magnificent hallway. It smelled of vinegar, clean and sharp, and the richer, rounder scent of beeswax. "You are Keeper of this house for the King?"

"And two others also within the palace grounds, Purgatory and Hell. As well as the palace itself, which includes the King's personal treasury." Again, that ironic tone.

"You choose to keep your rooms in Paradise, though?"

He laughed. "No one has ever commented on that before. I don't know whether to run screaming from you, Mistress Horenbout, or marry you forthwith."

Susanna spun toward him, surprised.

He was leaning back against the door, arms crossed over his chest, watching her in a way that made the hairs on her arms prickle as they had earlier with the King.

Then he straightened and walked toward the staircase that swept upward to a large landing. "Call me superstitious, but I'd rather live in Paradise than Purgatory."

"The King stays in these houses when he is in residence at Westminster?" She grasped the banister and hauled herself up the stairs after him.

Parker shook his head. "No. He used to use the main palace, but it caught fire a few years ago. His royal chambers were badly damaged, so he moved his official seat to Bridewell. These houses are used for his courtiers or for foreign dignitaries sometimes." He unlocked a door off the landing near the top of the stairs and walked in. Susanna stood at the threshold, looking into his chambers.

He pulled out a small trunk and began tossing clothes into it, along with ledgers and a sword, then closed and hefted the trunk easily in his arms.

No lackeys for this man. The time needed to find servants would have considerably lengthened their journey, but some courtiers would have insisted on finding them anyway.

Parker was a man not afraid to carry his own baggage.

She smiled at him.

He froze, then shook his head as if shaking himself awake.

"I know this has been a long day." He set the trunk down and stepped toward her, lifting a hand to her face. She saw it tremble before he ran a finger down her cheek.

His finger was so warm against her cold skin, she raised her own hand to press his more firmly in place.

His fingers tightened, sliding beneath her cap into her hair, and for a moment he cradled her head in his hand and looked into her eyes. Searching for something.

She would have given anything to know the question. To give the answer.

Someone whistled, sharp and piercing, below the window, and Parker drew back, his face neutral again.

"The barge pilot grows impatient." He scooped up the trunk again and held it between them as a bear tamer might hold a chair between himself and his animal—although who was being protected from whom, she didn't know.

"One more journey and we will be home?" she asked.

Parker gave her a strange look as he lifted the trunk onto his shoulder. "Aye. We will be home."

6

The Chiefe Conditions and Qualities in a Courtier:
Not to be a babbler, brauler, or chatter, nor lavish of
his tunge.

*Of the Chief Conditions and Qualityes in a Waytyng
Gentylwoman:* To drawe and peinct.

The pilot berthed at Old Swan, just short of London
Bridge. The rain had not let up, and the dark clouds
added to the gloom of a winter dusk. Parker could barely make
out the pier.

After he'd hauled their trunks from the barge, he lifted the
lantern and its flickering glow illuminated Susanna's shuttered
face, her eyes closed against the sting of the ice-laden rain.
She must regret the day she'd left Ghent.

With a loud whistle, Parker summoned the boys who huddled under the pier, waiting for the chance to carry bags or
beg. They were slow to respond, but at last one poked his head
out to see if there was a chance of earning a crust.

Parker held up four fingers, and four ragged figures scrambled up onto the wooden boards of Old Swan, shivering against the freezing rain.

They came forward reluctantly. One of the lads, the smallest one, stopped altogether, and Parker felt a prick of warning along the back of his neck.

The boy looked nervously at his companions, then moved forward again, and Parker saw the way the lad in front drew up, as if steeling himself.

Parker raised his lantern, and the light glinted off something sharp in the boy's hand.

"My lady!" he shouted, but his warning was drowned out in the cacophony of a thousand icicles hitting the wooden pier. He leaped forward and grabbed her with one arm around her waist, the other still holding the lantern up to see the boy. He caught a glimpse of a lifted arm, a few lurching steps, and swung Susanna behind him and turned back to face them.

The boys stumbled to a halt as Parker set the lantern down and pulled his knife from his boot. He drew his sword with the other hand, rolling his shoulders in anticipation of the fight.

The boy with the knife was so out of his depth, he froze, eyes wide and mouth slack as his companions scattered. The brief, roaring rage in Parker subsided to a howl.

He pounced, flicking the knife out of the boy's hand with his sword, and grabbed him around the throat.

"Who paid you?" He shook the lad at every word, then half-turned, his knife raised, as someone touched his arm.

Susanna looked back at him, eyes wide, whole body shivering.

"Bring him with us." Her lips were blue and stiff and he could see she was near collapse, her hand on his arm clinging for dear life.

He raised his head and was surprised to see that one of the boys lingered nearby, the youngest one who had held back earlier. Parker crooked a finger and, careful to stay out of reach, the boy came closer.

"Run to Orchard Cottage in Crooked Lane. Tell Mistress Greene to send round the cart. And to hurry."

The boy's mouth turned mulish and his eyes slid to the lad in Parker's grasp. "Why should I?"

"Because you want to see your brother again, alive and well." Parker had to shout over the rain, and the boy's eyes widened. "Now, go."

"You know these children?" Susanna asked as the boy disappeared into the night.

Parker shook his head, looked down at the older brother. "The only reason the boy would stay was for kin. The rest cleared out fast enough."

Susanna held herself tight, and he noticed that much of her hair had escaped its hood and was plastered against her cheeks. Her body flinched with every new gust of rain that battered them.

He strained to see up the road, and at last made out the flicker of a lantern. When the cart came into view, Parker saw with surprise that Mistress Greene herself was driving.

"Ho, there, Master Parker. Bit o' trouble?"

"Just a bit, Mistress Greene. Where is Luke?"

His housekeeper tossed her head. "Lad's run off on me, and I don't expect to see him back."

Parker pushed his captive toward the cart, then lifted him by his collar and set him beside Mistress Greene on the driver's seat. "Hold on to this devil for me, will you? And mind you get a good hold; I don't want to have to run after him."

Mistress Greene took charge, and Parker turned his attention to Susanna, lifting her up into the back of the cart and then hefting the trunks after her.

Finally, he grabbed the younger brother, who'd come skulking along behind the cart, and patted his clothes for any hidden weapons. He felt nothing but the sharp contours of the boy's ribs through the coarse sacking he wore.

"No need for that, m'lord." The boy's indignation made no impression on Parker. He stared the child down for a hard second, then lifted him into the back, where the lad scrambled into a corner and curled up against one of the trunks.

Parker pulled himself up next to Mistress Greene, and took hold of his captive once more.

The boy looked up at Parker, his eyes huge in his thin face. "What are you going to do to me, sir?"

"Make you sorry you were ever born."

———————

The fire in Parker's hearth fanned Susanna with its heat. Wave upon delicious wave of hot air beat against her cheeks, and she closed her eyes in pleasure.

She had changed out of her soaking clothes into one of the

dry dresses from her trunk, and she could feel her loose hair drying out in the warmth of the study, springing back in small curls around her temples.

Mistress Greene was off in the kitchen, ladling beef soup into bowls for them all, and Parker had given each of the boys one of his shirts. They stood before the fire with the fine cotton hanging to their knees, which made them look even younger and thinner than before.

Susanna studied the older boy—her would-be assassin. It defied imagination that he could be a killer, yet she had seen the knife raised in his hand with her own eyes.

She turned back to Parker, standing at his desk, and saw he watched them all with the blank, shuttered expression he used when he was thinking deeply.

"You have some explaining to do, boy."

The lad's face paled despite the heat of the fire. "Sir, I know it, but I beg of you, let my brother go. He weren't part of it."

"I don't think he would go, even if I gave him the choice," Parker said, and the younger boy shook his head. "Let's start with your names then."

With a sigh of capitulation, and a last frustrated look at his younger sibling, the lad rubbed his face with his hand. "I'm Peter Jack, sir, and my brother's Eric."

"Well then, Peter Jack. What have you against my lady that you wish her harm?"

Startled, Susanna jerked her gaze to Parker's face. His lady?

Peter Jack stood straight and turned to her. "You did me no

wrong, m'lady. I was paid to attack you. But my heart weren't in it." He seemed ashamed he was not yet a hardened criminal.

"You can rest assured that the only reason you are standing here with breath in your body is your reluctance for the work, Peter Jack." Parker crossed his hands over his chest. "Else I'd have done more with my sword than flick that knife into the river."

Knowing what he could have done, believing absolutely that Parker would have killed him had he thought Peter Jack had the nerve to follow through, brought home to her how dangerous Parker was. He was as cold-blooded as he needed to be.

Peter Jack seemed to realize it too, and he swallowed and stared hard at his bare feet. Eric reached across and took his arm, as if to confirm that his brother was beside him, alive and well.

Parker moved forward and both boys flinched, but he only eased himself into the chair set at an angle to Susanna's, facing the fire. "So who paid you?"

Peter Jack shrugged. "In this weather, in the dark, with the hood of his cloak over his head?" He lifted his hands at the impossibility of it.

Parker merely stared at him, the planes of his face hard and unbending, and the silence dragged out, broken only by the pop and crack of the wood burning in the fire and the occasional hiss as a drop of icy rain fell down the chimney.

"What did he ask of you?"

"Said you'd be comin' with a lady. That I were to stab her in the heart and leg it."

"He knew you?"

Peter Jack shrugged. "Maybe he's seen me afore."

Parker shifted in his chair. "How did he pay you?"

"He gave me a shilling. Said the rest would come later."

"And how could you get it later? If you killed my lady before my eyes, did you think you could return to Old Swan? Ever?"

There was a long silence as Peter Jack seemed to grapple with the consequences of what he'd almost done.

"No, sir." His voice was a whisper. "It was just, this winter . . . it's been so cold. Cold enough you can hardly think. And Eric an' me an' the lads, we look out for each other. A whole sovereign he promised me. That would've gone a long way."

Parker let the silence stretch out again, while Susanna fought a lump in her throat. Peter Jack had been manipulated, but he wasn't the villain here.

It was Eric who broke. "I know him. He's a crook from round the docks." Eric didn't look at Peter Jack, only at Parker.

Parker nodded, still saying nothing. Susanna was out of her depth here, treading water in the thick of it.

"How d'you know him?" Peter Jack asked his brother.

"Seen him afore, haven't I?" Eric shrugged. "Sometimes you can get a spot o' work at the dock, or something falls, or gets forgotten. Never know your luck there."

"Who is he?" Parker leaned forward, but his voice was calm, unexcited.

Eric shook his head. "Never heard his name." He cocked his head, and Susanna could see his usual cheekiness returning. "Mostly he's working the ships coming from the Netherlands, the ones with rolls of cloth. But he's sellin' something on the side, too. I seen some high-ups down there, making out they're inspecting their goods unloading from the ships, but their eyes are always moving, moving, until they find him. Then it's a quick duck round a corner or into a warehouse, and they're away again."

"What do you think he's selling?"

Eric lifted his hands, palms up. "It's small, whatever it is. Could be anything at all."

Parker relaxed back in his chair, a black hawk on its perch, deceptively still. He rested his elbows on the wooden arms and steepled his fingers. "So it could."

7

The Chiefe Conditions and Qualities in a Courtier: To be able to alleage good, and probable reasons upon everie matter.

Of the Chief Conditions and Qualityes in a Waytyng Gentylwoman: To shape him that is oversaucie wyth her, or that hath small respecte in hys talke, suche an answere, that he maye well understande she is offended wyth hym.

Susanna had gone to bed. She'd barely been able to lift her spoon from her broth to her mouth, and Parker hadn't been surprised when she said her good nights. Mistress Greene had insisted on helping her, closing the door behind her as they left. She would soon be back to put the boys in Luke's old room under the stairs in the kitchen, and he wanted to talk to Peter Jack without either woman present.

"It seems Mistress Greene is looking for a new groom and general helper," he said, and watched Peter Jack turn in his seat by the fire and stare at him.

Eric was fast asleep, sitting straight up, legs crossed. His toes peeped out beneath the shirt Parker had given him.

And he'd thought he'd had it bad as a lad. These boys knew the meaning of a hard life.

He held Peter Jack's gaze. "I need to trust the person who gets the job."

"You can trust me, sir. Honest." Peter Jack turned fully to face him, his eyes enormous, earnest.

"Who among your lads might have turned on you, Peter Jack?" Parker watched the boy swallow hard and look away. He hadn't expected a test of loyalty so soon.

They both knew Eric's man from the docks hadn't just been lucky. Someone had told him about the boys under Old Swan, told him Parker landed there to get home. The weapon might have been a desperate boy, but another hand had pointed him in Parker's direction.

Peter Jack opened his mouth, closed it, cleared his throat. He looked down, twining his fingers together. "Kinnock." The word came out strangled. At last he raised his head. "Kinnock's been actin' strange. I thought I seen him buy a pie the other day. A pie! He laughed and asked where'd he get the money for a pie. But I know I seen him."

"So, money from somewhere. That does point to him. They think he's useful where he is and didn't want him to have to disappear, so they picked someone else at random to do the job. Or Kinnock told them to choose you, because you're his competition. No matter—they know I'd hunt down whoever tried to hurt her, with the full backing of the King."

At Parker's mention of the King, a full-body shiver wracked Peter Jack's thin frame. He said nothing, but Parker saw he finally realized the trouble he'd gotten himself into.

"When did he start acting strange?"

Peter Jack frowned. "Couple o' days back. Well, stranger'n usual."

"And the rest of the lads?"

Peter Jack pulled himself together. "They're all right. They'd take me over Kinnock any day."

"Well then, we'll have to do something about Kinnock." Parker tapped his lips with his fingers. "And you can tell the lads I have some work for them too."

"What kind o' work?" Peter Jack crossed his arms over his chest and hugged himself tight.

"The King thinks I'm too straight," Parker replied. "But we're about to see how crooked I can be."

———

Parker was gone when Susanna woke the next morning and found Mistress Greene at work in the kitchen.

"Where are the lads?" She helped herself to the food Mistress Greene had left out for her.

"In the stables. It's a mess in there. Luke wasn't doing his work the last few days he was here, and then he walked off without so much as a by-your-leave."

Susanna lowered her mug of warm cider and swallowed a mouthful of bread. "Why did he leave?"

"Lazy." Mistress Greene punched into her dough, and kneaded it. "I expect someone to work if they're earning good money for it. And I see they have a warm place to sleep and a full belly as well as their wages. This ain't a bad place to lay your head."

Susanna caught the edge of sadness in Mistress Greene's tone. Bewilderment.

"It seems to me a lovely place to lay your head. I certainly slept well, and this bread and honey is delicious."

"Aye?" The housekeeper appeared mollified. "Well, I do keep a good house. And we're lucky to have the bread oven. Not many's got one around here."

"The journey last night was so dark and cold, I haven't even seen the house properly." Susanna stood and swept the crumbs she'd made on the table onto her plate. "I'd like a quick look before the weather worsens again."

"You do that. 'Twill snow before the day is out, mark my words."

Susanna fetched her cloak and stepped out into the yard, reluctantly closing off the heat of the kitchen behind her. The air was icy, stinging her cheeks, and she drew her cloak tighter. The clouds were tinged green, hanging low on the horizon. She felt hemmed in by them.

She made for the arch that led to the lane, wanting to get a better look at the street. She'd caught a glimpse of it from her bedroom window, and she was intrigued by the church at the top of the lane. She picked her way between the puddles and slush on the gravel-covered earth, grateful for her thick clogs.

Before stepping into the street, she turned to look back at Parker's house. It was an old two-story gray stone building with a thatch roof. Solid. Imposing. Her new home for a while.

For just a moment, she thought with longing of her home in Ghent: tall, elegant, with its beautiful murals decorating the exterior—some of her father's best work.

She had exiled herself from that. Or been exiled.

Her parents thought she'd given everything up for lust. But she hadn't. She'd gambled her father would allow her the same freedom he did Lucas. Afford her the same respect. But she had lost.

Her chances of marriage were slim if she continued as an artist, and she had no plans to become a nun. She thought of Joost, and shivered. But her father had not placed her . . . explorations with Joost in the same category as Lucas's affairs. Instead, he'd shipped her off to England, throwing her to the wolves.

But that wasn't fair. None of this madness in England was her father's fault.

With a sigh, Susanna turned toward the street. The cold was making her feet ache, and she needed to move. She stepped through the arch and turned, colliding with a man lurking just outside against the wall.

He was big in a rawboned, gangly way, his arms and legs too long for his body, his hands huge. He grunted as Susanna hit him, but kept his footing.

A cry of surprise caught in her throat. The man had a wild-eyed, unpredictable look, like a wounded animal, and she took an instinctive step back.

His cap had long sides to cover his ears and he wore gray homespun cloth, his shoes just leather soles wrapped in cloth. He lurched forward, something desperate in the movement, and Susanna turned and began to run across the yard.

His hand reached out, caught hold of her cloak, and yanked her back.

She went down with a scream, landing on her back in the wet mud of the courtyard, the wind knocked out of her. She lay gasping for breath as he loomed over her, blocking out the sky.

"Get back!" Peter Jack called out, his voice deeper somehow, fierce. "Get back from her."

The man started, shuffled back a little, and Susanna saw Peter Jack and Eric standing at the barn door. Peter Jack had a pitchfork in his hands, and Eric wielded an axe that was half his height. They would barely reach her attacker's midriff.

"Oi!" Mistress Greene burst from the back door, wielding a rolling pin in one hand and a saucepan in the other.

The man crouched at Susanna's head, his breath coming faster, his eyes flicking between the boys and Mistress Greene. There was a knife in his hand. Susanna saw its dull glint as he lowered it to her throat.

"No!" Peter Jack charged, pitchfork raised, at the same moment Susanna rolled away.

The man jerked the knife sideways, catching the cord of

her cloak. He cursed in panic when the blade wouldn't come free, and in desperation, yanked it hard, cutting the cord and nicking Susanna under her chin.

Somehow the cloak was tangled around his arm, and with a tug he pulled it out from under her and was up and running. Susanna rolled to her stomach in time to see him disappear around the corner, her cloak clutched tightly in one hand, his knife held high in the other.

She pushed herself up on her knees, wincing.

"That was fast work," Peter Jack said, holding out a hand to help her up.

"Fast work?"

"I didn't finish ye off last night, so they sent someone round next day to do it."

"What on earth?" Mistress Greene arrived in her rolled-up sleeves and her apron, flour on her cheek. "What was that about?"

"Got a price on her 'ead, this one," Eric told her, jerking his head toward Susanna.

"Go on." Mistress Greene looked at each of them, and Susanna saw her mouth close with a snap as she realized they were serious. She looked out into the lane. "Well, we saw him off, didn't we?"

"Course we did. What with bein' armed to the teeth 'n' all," Eric said, looking at her saucepan and rolling pin as he leaned on his axe handle.

It set them all off laughing. Susanna felt tears on her

cheeks. She clutched her stomach, felt the ache of her back where she'd fallen. Saw the blood drip from her chin to mingle with the dirty water she was standing in.

That was how Parker found them, howling with laughter, near hysteria, standing without coats or cloaks in the middle of his yard.

8

The Chiefe Conditions and Qualities in a Courtier: Not to renn, wrastle, leape, nor cast the stone or barr with men of the Countrey, except he be sure to gete the victorie.

Of the Chief Conditions and Qualityes in a Waytyng Gentylwoman: To be esteamed no lesse chast, wise and courteous, then pleasant, feat conceited and sober.

Susanna and Parker stood before the Boar's Head public house. It looked warm and inviting, especially now the snow had started. Thick, fat flakes drifted down, each feather-light touch to her cheeks and neck an icy kiss as they melted on her skin.

"The vestry business of St. Michael's is conducted in a tavern?" she asked Parker dubiously.

He slanted her a look, still barely controlling his anger at the latest attempt on her life. She suspected he blamed it on her. "St. Michael's is the livery church of the Worshipful Company of Plumbers. The company prefers meeting here with the parish priests. It's warmer than the vestry and there is more space."

He looked up and down Crooked Lane and, satisfied the street was clear of assassins for the time being, opened the heavy wooden door of the tavern.

Susanna stepped forward, but he shook his head. "They could have someone planted in the Boar's Head, for all I know." There was an edge to his voice, sharp as a stiletto.

If there was someone biding his time on the other side of the door, waiting to kill her, she felt sorry for him. Parker would show no mercy, parish priests as an audience or no. The veneer of civility, the fine outer layer of the courtier, had been worn down. Worn through. The real Parker lurked just below the surface.

She shivered, and this time it wasn't because of the snow.

She noticed a flick of his right hand, and saw his blade drop into his palm before he stepped inside.

He held the door for her, but his eyes swept the room.

"Master Parker!"

The priest who hailed him was sitting at a long table with eight or nine other men. All had tankards of ale and bread and cheese before them. A large wooden bowl of apples had been pushed to one side, their red-green skins like gems against the black clerical robes. A fire roared in a massive fireplace behind them.

Susanna sighed. This was a scene she did not need to subvert. Priests sitting easily with a group of plumbers in a pub—it was perfect.

"Father Haden." Parker made his way to the priest, his hand firmly on Susanna's arm.

She smiled at them all, holding the painting as it would be firmly in her mind.

"Who is this lovely lady with you, Parker?" Another priest, his light blue eyes glinting in the glow of the fire, stood and bowed to her. The other men followed his lead with a scrape of chairs.

"We don't see him for weeks on end, and then he appears with a beauty on his arm. Ho-ho, Parker, you are a dark one." The man who spoke was no priest. Susanna could tell by his clothes and his hands, which had seen enough hard labor to scar and mark them. She placed him in the painting, leaning on his elbows, his head thrown back in a laugh, his hands resting easily on either side of his mug.

"Gentlemen." Parker bowed, showing no reaction to the lighthearted teasing. "Father Haden, if we may have a private word?"

A look passed among the men, and they sat again, watching Parker carefully, their faces alight with curiosity about Susanna.

Father Haden rose slowly under the weight of his old bones, and Parker drew him aside. "I would present Mistress Susanna Horenbout, Father. She is the King's painter, newly come from Ghent."

"Horenbout?" Father Haden cast her a swift glance. His body was bent with age, but his energy was undiminished. A lively fire burned in his dark brown eyes, and his white hair, though clipped into submission, looked as though it had a life of its own. "I have heard of Horenbout. Gerard Horenbout painted the portraits of the King for the glass windows at St. Nicholas in Calais."

"You have seen them, sir?" Susanna asked him.

"Aye. I made a small journey some years ago."

"Gerard Horenbout is my father."

"Well, it is a pleasure to meet you, mistress."

Parker's mouth was a hard line. He was clearly impatient to get on, to take action. And he could take no action unless she was safe.

"There is something afoot at court, Father." Parker's voice dropped so low, both Susanna and the priest had to lean forward to hear him. "Mistress Horenbout has been caught up in it, and the King has set me the task of ensuring her safety."

Father Haden kept silent, waiting for Parker to explain.

"An attack was made on her in my own courtyard not two hours past, and I have a suspicion who it may have been. But I cannot leave her alone again, and I ask if she can be part of your company in the tavern this afternoon."

"We are not trained soldiers, Parker."

Parker shrugged. "There are ten of you. And some of the plumbers are able enough. Master Selby alone would give an attacker pause."

"Surely you have the full guard of the King at your disposal?"

"Aye. And not a one could I trust in this matter."

Father Haden looked grave. "That is the way of it, then?" He watched Parker's face, then gave a decisive nod. "Of course Mistress Horenbout is welcome to sit with us."

"Father." Susanna placed a hand on the old priest's arm. "Would it be rude of me to paint you instead? You make such a wonderful scene, all sitting at the table."

Father Haden laughed. "Well now, I never would have said we were pretty as a picture. But if that is what you want."

She nodded, her hand already inside her bag, touching the small oak panel within. She had not known what to expect in England on her arrival, had not known if the King would require immediate work, so she had a panel already primed and plenty of ground pigment for her paints.

"I can see the light of inspiration in your eyes, Mistress Horenbout. And I am not one to stand in its way. Let me introduce you to the others, and then you can begin painting some old men at rest."

As he took her arm, Parker reached out and held her shoulder. "Do not leave the tavern. For any reason. I'll be back as soon as I can."

"Take care." Susanna touched his hand with a light brush of her fingertips, and blinked at the spark she felt. She saw something flare deep in Parker's eyes, then deepen even more when he noticed her reaction.

Parker took a step back, and her hand fell to her side. "It is not I who needs to be on guard today," he answered, his voice rough. He sketched a salute to the priest, then dipped a quick bow to the rest of the table.

As he walked toward the door, Susanna noticed the blade had never left his hand.

T he docks. It kept leading back to the docks. His old
     haunting ground.

Parker counted the connections as he dodged a cart piled
with fish, the cartman swearing as he strained to push it over
the potholes in the cobbled street. First Harvey, a merchant
and spy who'd gleaned most of his secrets in harbor taverns.
Then Eric's man, the mysterious dockhand. And now Gripper.

Halfway through Susanna's description of the attack,
Parker had known it was Gripper. It had to be.

The worm would expect Parker to come after him, and
would be hiding in the darkest sewer he could find.

And Parker knew just where that sewer was. He'd hidden
there himself a time or two. Before fate had intervened and
taken him from pauper to gentleman. One of the King's new
men, as Norfolk contemptuously called them. No pedigree but
their own efficiency and intelligence.

Parker thought there could be no higher compliment—not
that Norfolk had the wit to realize it.

"Master Parker. Roughin' it, are ye? Miss the stews?"

Parker stopped short and turned to the figure huddled
against a wooden warehouse wall. She was wrapped in so
many rag layers, she resembled a hessian sack. "Mistress Goodnight." Parker bowed, and heard the old crone cackle with delight. "I would hardly call the docks the stews."

"Then ye'd be blind." She shuffled away from the wall and

hunched as the wind tugged at her wrappings. "Lookin' for Gripper?"

Parker hid his reaction, but he couldn't fool her. There was a gleam of triumph in Gladys Goodnight's eyes.

"Naught c'n get a fright into that lump like you, Master Parker. And he ran like the six divils of hell were after him when he came past."

Parker nodded slowly in understanding. "Clutching a cloak in his hand?"

"Ye always was a quick 'un, Parker. Aye, winter is that bitter and I'm not for much longer lest something changes. Like I gets me a new cloak."

Parker slipped a hand into his money pouch and brought out a sovereign.

Gladys squawked like a chicken. "Just the cloak'll do it."

"The cloak *and* this, Mistress Goodnight. My business with Gripper is . . . urgent."

"Eh?" For the first time, Gladys looked worried. "You ain't going to really kill 'im, is yer?"

Parker shrugged. He wouldn't lie. Killing Gripper would be more satisfying than a shipload of new crossbows.

"Thing is . . ." Gladys shuffled on the spot. "I can't be party to killin' one o' their own, Parker. They'd be stickin' the knife in me 'fore your back is turned."

"They?"

"Strange sorts around the docks these days. 'Tain't wise to provoke 'em." Gladys sniffed, then wiped her nose on a filthy sleeve. "Ruthless, they are."

"And Gripper is in league with them?" The freezing wind seemed to claw into his bones, but he waited patiently.

Gladys laughed. "You always spoke fancy, even when you spent yer afternoons here as a lad, but now you're right royalty. Gripper's in league wif 'em, all right. In league." She sniggered.

"So where is he?"

Gladys weighed the scales, and must have decided Parker wouldn't kill Gripper. "Hidin' in back o' the Squealin' Pig."

Well, well, well. Gripper had changed his hidey-hole—from a sewer to a pub that served the contents of a sewer.

Parker turned on his heel, lifting his hand in a wave of thanks. He hadn't seen Gripper in—could it be nearly a year? He'd been busier for the King than he'd realized. And that old life was slipping away.

It hadn't been much of a life. He hadn't fitted in on the docks, either. He'd been from too good a family.

Parker would have smiled at the irony, but the wind had frozen his face to stone.

He ducked around the corner of the Squealing Pig and made his way up the dank alley that ran between it and a warehouse storing cured hides, by the stink of it.

The back door to the Squealing Pig was propped open with a half-brick, just enough to let out the steam and smoke from the cooking without losing too much of the heat.

Parker stepped inside, taking it all in at once. There was a clatter of dishes to the left and the vibrating twang of spoons against copper pots. He saw two girls and an old woman stirring stew and stacking bowls. Gripper wasn't in sight, and Parker eased along the wall, as yet unseen.

There was a door off the kitchen, partly open, and as he drew closer Parker could hear the buzz of conversation from within.

Nothing like the advantage of surprise.

He gripped his blade and exploded into the room. The door bounced off the wall and slammed closed behind him.

Gripper and two other men looked up at him from a small table, eyes wide. Parker reached forward and grabbed Gripper, lifting him from his chair and snaking his arm forward so his knife came to rest on the left side of Gripper's throat, just under his ear.

"Good day, Gripper."

Gripper went stiff with fear. "Parker."

"Now, why are you holed up in a tavern playing one-and-thirty when you should be on your knees in church after what you got up to today, eh?"

"I'm that sorry, Parker," Gripper whined, glancing across to his companions, who now stood huddled against the far wall of the tiny closet.

Parker smiled. He had Gripper in an extremely difficult position.

He couldn't apologize to Parker without losing face. But Parker's knife was digging into the soft skin under his chin.

Parker waited to see what he would do.

"Let my friends go, at least," Gripper said at last.

"So they can call reinforcements? I don't think so, Gripper." Parker applied a slight pressure to the knife.

"Ow. No. What do you want?"

"You have done some stupid things through the years, Gripper, but attacking someone under my protection on my own property?"

Gripper swallowed, his Adam's apple bobbing against the sharp edge of the blade. "I had no choice." His voice was a whisper, and Parker bent to hear him better. "Someone needed her dead, and I knew the lay o' the land."

"Why do they need her dead, Gripper?"

Gripper was silent, his eyes closed, his body trembling.

He wasn't going to answer.

He'd given himself up for dead at Parker's hand, which told Parker he'd decided he was a dead man either way, and Parker's way would be the less painful one.

Parker pushed the thirst for revenge aside. He'd love to put the worm out of his misery, but they'd keep sending people to kill Susanna. Until he knew why, he couldn't make it stop. And for all his vigilance, someone just might get lucky.

Gripper almost had.

He needed to get him alone. In a way that made these other two louts believe talking was the last thing on Parker's mind.

"I'm going to kill you, Gripper," he said, and he lifted him by the neck and swung back his knife hand to open the door.

Gripper was fighting for air, his hands clawing at Parker's arm as they backed through the kitchen, his heels kicking uselessly against the floor as Parker pulled him along.

"Keep still, you idiot," Parker hissed in his ear. "I'm not really going to kill you." He hauled Gripper over the threshold and dragged him down the steps. "At least, not yet."

9

The Chiefe Conditions and Qualities in a Courtier: No lyer.

Of the Chief Conditions and Qualityes in a Waytyng Gentylwoman: To do the exercises meete for women, comlye and with a good grace.

Gripper fought him all the way, until eventually Parker cuffed him. Hard.

Gripper had never been anything but trouble. And he'd never failed to betray Parker. Since the beginning of their association, if there was one thing Parker could count on, it was for Gripper to lie or deceive him in some way.

The first time, it had near killed him. He'd never been taken in again, although Gripper had tried.

Gripper suddenly bit down on Parker's hand and, losing patience, losing all sense of restraint, Parker threw him into the back alley he'd chosen for his interrogation.

He heard Gripper's head smack against the wall as he tumbled to the ground, and the groan he gave was genuine.

Good.

Parker drew his sword and gently touched the tip to the hollow of Gripper's throat as he sat up.

Gripper shook his head, blinked, and then looked bleakly down at the sword.

"They'll kill me, Parker. Honest. They will." The fight went out of him.

"And I won't?" Parker flicked the sword up to tap Gripper under the chin, forcing the man to look him in the eye, then rested the tip back at his throat.

Gripper shrugged. "If I die by your sword, it won't hurt. They'll do it slow and hard, call it a lesson to others or summat."

"Gripper, you are a bastard." Parker gritted his teeth, hating what he was about to say. "But I can make you disappear. They can think I killed you. And when I have every one of them at the gallows, you can return."

"What's the price?" Gripper sniffed and looked at him from under his bushy brows.

"Who are they?"

"Dunno." Gripper gave a little shriek as Parker pierced his skin and drew blood. "I swear, I don't know. They're dock-hands. Got a bit going on the side. Some o' the merchandise falls out o' its barrel, they profit."

"They don't sound very organized. What do they want with you?"

"I know what's what around here. All the good hiding places. And I can shift the stuff sometimes."

"And this morning?"

Gripper pulled his legs up to his chest, careful to keep his neck still. "Said they'd heard I knew you. Knew where you lived an' all."

"So you grabbed up a knife and went off to kill a woman, just like that?"

Some of what he was feeling must have come through in his voice, because Gripper went very still.

"I thought . . . thought it'd be easy. I didn't know her. And the money was . . . good." He swallowed. "Then she lay there, trying to breathe, and those boys and your cook—all shouting at me. . . ." He shuddered, and the sword dug into his skin. Gripper whimpered.

"You must have known what I'd do."

"Waited for you to leave, din't I? Waited for me chance. Thought she'd be dead and you'd never know who done it."

"Who asked you to do the job?"

"One o' the lads back at the Pig, Rhys. But it weren't for him. 'Twere for someone else."

"Who?" Parker could almost taste it. He was finally getting somewhere.

"Dunno. Some cove. If he wants a job doing, he'll sneak up on you in the dark to ask you. Always wears a hooded cloak."

"Damn it, Gripper. Give me something!"

Gripper cringed, then Parker saw the moment a thought slid into his head, turning his expression from fearful to sly.

"I do have one thing."

"Well?"

"He hates you, Parker. Whoever set this up."

"How do you know that?" Parker slowly eased the sword away from Gripper's throat.

"The man what gave Rhys the job, he said the fee would triple if Rhys sent you to the divil as well."

"Why did Rhys give the job to you? You could have shown him the way for a small cut."

There was a sound behind him, and Parker turned, keeping Gripper in view.

Rhys stood blocking the way, his friend behind him. Both held knives.

"I didn't want to be seen killing one o' the King's new men at his own house. No money's worth that." Rhys gave Parker a cold smile. "But seeing as ye obliged and put yourself in this alley, I might just try me hand at it."

Parker weighed the odds. He was older and bigger than Rhys or his companion. But they were two against one, possibly three against one. Gripper could be counted on to wait and choose the winning side.

Rhys postured a moment, flicking his knife provocatively.

Another amateur.

Parker lifted his sword and his knife together, leaped forward, and lunged, felt the brief moment of resistance before the sword's tip pierced Rhys's belly. Before Rhys could even gasp, Parker's knife came up and across, slashing his throat.

With a sickening gurgle, Rhys went down, and his companion went from grinning to white-faced. He stumbled back, a keening note coming from his throat as he stared in horror at the widening pool of blood around Rhys.

Parker forced himself to move, to give this death some meaning. He leaped over the body, grabbed Rhys's companion, and yanked him back into the alley. The youth stepped on Rhys's hand as he was hauled forward, and a cry wrenched from his throat, his body limp with shock, unresisting.

Parker threw him onto the cobbles next to Gripper and lifted his bloodied sword. It was enough to get their full attention.

"Unless someone tells me something useful, I'm the only one who'll be leaving this alley alive."

————————

When she was this deep in a painting, time had no meaning.

Someone had put a mug of ale down for her, but even though she was thirsty, could feel a headache coming on from lack of drink, she couldn't put aside her brush to pick it up.

She was running out of paint, and she felt the thin, spidery touches of panic that her supply would not hold out.

She wanted to capture the feel, the play of light and shadow, the atmosphere. All the finer details could be added later. Only when she was this deep in the piece, in the moment, was the reality of it at one with the picture in her mind.

The men had long ago forgotten her. Or if they did send her interested glances now and then, they were no longer embarrassed or overconscious of her. No one had tried to look over her shoulder, and for that she was grateful. She would not like to cause offense by cuffing someone.

She'd smacked Lucas in the face once, and it had ruined the picture for her. He shouted so loudly with surprise, grabbing her arms, that her concentration had been entirely broken.

He'd never looked over her shoulder again, and she smiled in remembrance of the laughs they'd had after that, comparing stories of what they'd done while deep in work.

And still, with all that, with every other thing equal, her father thought she should not sleep with Joost. While Lucas could bed half of Ghent if he had a mind to.

Parker's face came to her and she tried to push it aside, regretting the train of her thoughts. They drew her away from the painting and she fought them, gently brushing the pale yellow of a fire's glow onto the sturdy mugs on the table, on the cheeks of those sitting closest to the flames.

Parker was much more interesting than Joost. More dangerous, more vital. More everything. And her father was not here to stop her.

She felt a tension deep within, a coiling of nerves and excitement. With an annoyed exclamation, she stepped back from the painting.

She shrugged her shoulders, rolled her neck, and felt the muscles contract and protest. Finally, she reached for her mug and savored the feel of rising from some deep, weightless place back into the real world.

With a blink she took in the deep darkness, the dwindled number of men at the table, the bang of the door as a new patron entered the Boar's Head.

Just how long had passed?

"Mistress Horenbout, I see you are back among us."

Father Haden stood at her elbow, and she started in surprise. How long had he been there, watching her?

"My apologies, Father. I am poor company when I feel a work this strongly. It absorbs me."

"May I see it?"

With a flick of panic, Susanna's eyes went to the painting, suddenly unsure of it.

It glowed back at her.

It was the first time she'd stepped back and looked at the small painting as a whole, the first clear look she'd had.

It was good. She felt the tremor of excitement unfurl within. As strong as the sexual pull a moment before at the thought of Parker.

No wonder so many artists slept with their models.

"It is not complete, but yes."

The priest stepped closer, squinting in the dying light to look. "Magnificent," he murmured.

His praise sparked requests from the other men; even the landlord and his wife asked to look. Soon there was a crowd around the easel, their voices hushed as if in church.

"If I hadn't seen yer there with me own eyes, painting it, I'd never believe 'twas a woman done it."

The landlord meant it as praise, but suddenly exhausted,

drained of all energy, Susanna was not able to summon even a weak smile at the insult.

She sat on the chair someone had drawn up for her and took another gulp of her ale. She was just lowering the mug when the door to the Boar's Head crashed open, blowing in snow and leaves and Parker.

His cloak billowed around him in the icy breeze before the door swung shut, and every voice was still as all eyes turned to look.

He was a warrior, cloaked in darkness. Even in the weak light of the lanterns and fire, her eye picked up the blood crusted on his knuckles, the look in his eyes that said he was fighting his way back from a dark pit.

Parker had left the Boar's Head this afternoon and, despite preferring paradise, had taken a trip to hell.

10

The Chiefe Conditions and Qualities in a Courtier: To be handesome and clenly in his apparaile.

Of the Chief Conditions and Qualityes in a Waytyng Gentylwoman: To apparaile her self so, that she seeme not fonde and fantasticall.

W hat happened?" Susanna asked softly the moment they entered the house. She hadn't dared say anything on the way home from the Boar's Head. Parker's expression was closed. He would not answer her on a public street.

"Too much." He took her cloak, and his fingers lingered on her shoulders. "Not enough."

"You were attacked?" She waited for him to turn back from hanging up her cloak, then took one of his hands in hers, rubbed a thumb over the blood that splattered the back of it.

"It was more a clash. A battlefield engagement." He withdrew his hand and clenched it as if ashamed. "They tried, but only I drew blood."

"There was more than one?"

Parker shrugged as if it didn't matter. "Three, if you count Gripper."

"Who is Gripper?"

"The ruffian who attacked you in the courtyard."

Susanna's eyes widened. "I count him."

"You know something of great importance, Susanna."

She couldn't remember when he'd stopped calling her Mistress Horenbout and begun addressing her so intimately, and she didn't care. "I have told you everything I know."

"That cannot be true—" He held up a hand as the protest exploded from her. "I believe you. There is something you do not realize you know."

She cocked her head to the side as her indignation subsided. "Else why would they still be so relentless?"

She led the way to the study and took the chair by the fire again, rubbing her hands close to the blaze. The house was strangely still. She wondered where Mistress Greene and the boys were.

"Aye. No one takes these kinds of risks without being desperate." Parker poked at the fire, threw on another log, and eased into the chair beside her. "But the risk is controlled. There are so many layers between the brains behind this and the blunt weapons he throws at us, I have barely scratched the surface of lies and confusion."

"Sending someone to kill me who was known to you was ill-thought."

Parker nodded. "The person behind this didn't employ

Gripper to attack you. The man he did hire got Gripper to come in his stead."

Susanna thought about that. "Then whoever sent Gripper will no doubt be in trouble himself now."

Parker scrubbed a hand over his face. "Where he has gone, that is the least of his worries."

She finally understood. "He is dead?"

"Aye."

The thin whistle of the wind through the gap between the window and its frame and the pop of the fire as snow drifted down the chimney were the only sounds. A sense of debt to Parker for what he had done, had been forced to do to protect them all, stole over her.

Reluctant to speak, reluctant to move, weighed down by death and dread, Susanna roused herself with an effort of will. "I know you are occupied with many other things, but I would like to call on Master Harvey's widow. She will wish to hear his last words."

Parker stiffened. He looked at her sharply, all regrets about recent events pushed aside. She could almost see his mind spinning, as suddenly hers spun as well.

Mistress Greene's shriek from the kitchen cut through her thoughts like a blade.

She leaped to her feet, but Parker reached the door before she'd taken two steps.

"Stay." The command was thrown over his shoulder as he charged ahead, sword and knife in his hands.

Susanna stood frozen, looking at the empty doorway, her stomach clenching.

The silence went on forever. Each creak and groan of the wooden boards beneath her feet, each pop and sizzle from the fire, stretched out interminably.

She could stand it no more, had to know what was afoot. She took a tentative step toward the door, then another. She paused just on the threshold.

What would she do if someone was attacking them? Had managed to attack Parker?

She looked back into the room and saw the brass poker in its fine filigree stand by the fireplace. She strode back, swung it up, and held it before her as she entered the passageway.

She crept forward, one cautious step at a time. A small rustle, a quiet groan, sounded behind the half-open kitchen door at the end of the passage, freezing her to the spot.

The groan came again and she slid along the wall, crouching down as she reached the door. She paused, listening intently, but it was unnaturally quiet.

She could not wait a moment longer.

She took a deep breath and stood, threw the door open with a crash, poker raised. At first it seemed no one was there, until she heard the muffled groan again.

Mistress Greene lay on her side before the fireplace, curled tight as a bud.

With a cry, Susanna flung herself down next to her, searching for injuries.

"Mistress Greene, where are you hurt?"

The housekeeper raised her head off the rush-strewn floor, and Susanna saw a small pool of blood beneath her, soaked up by the dried leaves. Blood smeared her cheek and had begun to dry in thick rivulets above her eyebrow.

"The boys?" she asked in a weak voice.

Susanna glanced around, but there was no sign of the boys. No sign of Parker, either.

He would never have left Mistress Greene to lie here if he'd seen her. So either he hadn't seen her, or . . .

Susanna stood.

Parker would not have gone quietly, and he would not have been easy to take.

She raised the poker again and crept to the back door. It was ajar, and the cold air flowed in, viscous and heavy.

The yard was empty. In the light from the lantern hanging above the stable door, she could see it was open, and from inside the stable Susanna could hear the thud and grunt of a fight.

She grabbed a pile of clean rags from the table and ran back to Mistress Greene, lifting her head gently and pillowing the cloths under it.

"Don't go to sleep," she whispered. "I'll be back in a moment."

As she returned to the back door, she saw the cleaver Mistress Greene used to chop chicken carcasses lying on the table. She picked it up and hefted it in her right hand, the poker in her left. Then she ran out into the yard, keeping an eye on the archway where Gripper had grabbed her that morning. No one lurked in the street that she could see.

She hovered around the stable entrance, trying to peer without getting too close to the door.

She saw a foot almost on the stable threshold. It was small, pathetic, illuminated by the wedge of lantern light that cut into the stable's gloom.

Eric.

Since she'd found Mistress Greene, a rage had been building at these people who would not stop coming. Who thought nothing of the lives they were destroying.

Her anger was cold as the air she breathed, and Eric's foot made the rage grow colder. Cold as a blizzard.

She ran through the door, stooped over double, and crouched next to Eric. He had been struck senseless, but she was relieved to hear him take a shuddering breath.

Peter Jack lay two feet away, his face a mess of bruises and cuts. His eyes fluttered open, stared at her blankly for a moment, then closed again.

She stood and heard the thump of a body against the wooden planks of the stable stall, a grunt of effort as flesh struck flesh.

Parker, who had already spent his day fighting for his life and for information to protect hers.

Enough was enough.

Furious, she hefted her weapons and made for the stall just as two men burst from it: Parker locked in battle with some tradesman or laborer, by his dress.

Blood streamed down their faces and matted their hair. The fine linen and velvet of Parker's clothes were as ripped and torn as his attacker's rough wool. Wild beasts fighting to the death.

They fell to the floor and Parker's attacker grabbed his head by the hair, lifted it up to crack it down on the wooden planks. The man drew back his lips in a snarl, and Susanna saw blood coating the whites of his teeth.

She ran forward, the poker already swinging down, and caught him a hard crack on the back of his head.

He grunted in pain and shot her a look of disbelief, then half-stood to come after her.

Parker rolled away and began to heave himself up, but his attacker shook his head as if to clear it and turned his attention back to Parker.

It had become personal for him, Susanna could see. She was the only one armed with anything more than fists, she was the only one standing on her feet—but he dismissed her out of hand as a threat.

His mistake.

With a cry, she rushed him, swinging the cleaver and the poker together. He turned and blocked the poker's blow just in time, flicking it from her hand.

He didn't even see the cleaver.

Susanna heard the thud of metal into flesh, felt the vibration down the wooden handle in her hand.

She'd never heard a more horrendous noise. Felt a more terrible sensation.

Bile rose in her throat and she stumbled back, blinking at the sight of the cleaver buried deep in the fleshy part of his right upper arm.

She tripped backward, fell to the floor, the world suddenly all white and strange, filled with a buzzing noise and tiny colored lights.

She dipped her head to her knees, panting, knowing she could not afford to faint.

Up. She had to get up.

She moved to her hands and knees, finally got her feet under her and stood, swaying.

"You bitch!" The attacker had lost his startled expression, replaced by outrage and venom. He braced himself and pulled the cleaver from his arm.

The blood gushed and spurted from the wound as if it would use up every drop in his body.

"I'm going to kill you." He took a step forward, but his footing was unsteady, his eyes unfocused and dazed.

Fear ripped her from her fog. Susanna looked for Parker and saw him standing at last, breathing deeply. As the attacker took another faltering step, Parker lurched forward and shoved him over.

The man went down without a sound and lay still, looking up at the open beams of the stable ceiling.

"We need to stop the bleeding," Parker said, and he pulled off his tattered sleeves, ripping them from their laces.

He bent down to their attacker and Susanna knelt beside

him. Smelled the sweat and blood and rage coming off Parker, mingled with the sweet barn scent of hay and horse.

"I don't want this one to die," Parker said as he tightened his sleeve around the wound.

"You want to question him?" Susanna looked at the man's face, white and clammy with sweat. "Will he talk?"

Parker turned to her, touched a bloodstained finger to her cheek. "He will when I'm through with him."

————————

You use your right and left hands equally well." Parker watched as Susanna bathed Eric's head wound. "A good person to have in a fight."

She shrugged. "I was born favoring my left hand." Her mouth turned up in a humorless smile, and he realized she must have been taught to use her right hand because of the stigma attached to using the left.

"My father and brother too." Her smile turned genuine. "They would have been more use to you, no doubt. I faint at the first blow struck."

"You are no warrior, and there is no shame in that. You struck your blow, no matter what you did afterward. The outcome could have been much different without Mistress Greene's cleaver and your aim."

She shook her head. "You were getting to your feet, Parker. You would have overcome him."

"I might have overcome him, I might not have. When I

entered the kitchen and chased the ruffian out, I had no notion there were two of them." He should have anticipated that they would up the stakes. The man had led him straight to the barn and into a trap. His fist clenched so tightly on the damp cloth he held that a trickle of water ran down his forearm.

Susanna gasped and put down the cloth she was using on Eric. "There were two? What happened to the other one?"

"Dead. Lying somewhere in the hay of the stable with my knife in him." That reminded him, he needed to retrieve it. And his sword.

He had never been disarmed in a fight before. Never been taken so much by surprise.

He flicked his gaze over Eric and Peter Jack, lying still and pale on their beds. He had helped Susanna put Mistress Greene to bed, and now they were tending to the boys.

There was movement behind them, someone pushing open the back door, and Parker spun to meet the new threat.

"Parker?" The woman standing there started, putting out a hand to steady herself against the door frame, a look of fear on her face. "I came as quick as I could."

"Your pardon, Maggie." He must look bad if Maggie blanched at the sight of him. He'd once seen her wade into a brawl to help an injured man.

She patted her heart. "Thought you were about to set upon me."

He shook his head. "I thought the ruffians had returned."

"No matter. Where are my patients?" She stepped fully into the room, and Parker spied her shy little apprentice, carrying some of the satchels full of herbs and ointments the healer used. She was a thin, sylphlike figure with golden hair, a fairy to Maggie's hag.

"Mistress Greene is in her chamber, through this door and to the right. The boys are in here." He gestured to the little room behind him and saw Susanna standing in the doorway.

"M'lady." Maggie curtsied, and her apprentice shadowed her action.

Parker tried to see Susanna through their eyes. Her gown was fine wool, her shoes of fine leather. But there the resemblance to a lady ended. Her cheek was smudged with blood, and with a start, Parker recalled stroking it earlier with his bloody fingers. Her cap was missing, and her hair tumbled wild around her shoulders.

"Please." Susanna stepped forward, holding out her hands. "Tell me how I can help you. Anything you need, I will do."

Maggie nodded in approval. "I'll check the patients and give ye my list."

Parker noted with relief that he was no longer needed. He bowed. "Ladies, there are things I must attend to in the stable."

Susanna looked at him sharply, her eyes wide.

"We no longer have time for pity, my lady," he said, knowing she was thinking of what he was prepared to do to get answers.

She hesitated a moment, then her gaze fell on the boys' still, white faces. She nodded.

He turned and walked out into the yard, his pace steady.

He had never had much use for pity, even before he became a leashed wolf for the King. Now he had gnawed through his tether, and the wolf was running wild.

11

The Chiefe Conditions and Qualities in a Courtier: To
consider whom he doth taunt and where: for he
ought not to mocke poore seelie soules, nor men of
authoritie, nor commune ribaldes and persons given
to mischeef, which deserve punishment.

*Of the Chief Conditions and Qualityes in a Waytyng
Gentylwoman:* Not to speake woordes of dishon-
estye and baudrye to showe her self pleasant, free
and a good felowe.

He saw to his knife and his sword first; he felt naked
without them.

Then he turned back to the injured attacker, propped up
against a bale of straw, his legs tied securely to the center support of the stable. The man was sliding into shock. He was
shivering violently, and his face felt cold and clammy to the
touch.

Parker threw a horse blanket over him and gave his cheek
a little tap.

"Huh?" The man turned blindly to face him, fighting to
open his eyes.

"You the one who set the wharf boys on my lady last night?"

The man mumbled something unintelligible, and Parker gave his cheek a sharp slap.

"Wha . . . ?"

"Do you want to live?" He could hear the exhaustion in his own voice. The raw honesty.

The man's eyes tried to focus on Parker's face. "Nearly gone anyway."

Parker lifted his knife and moved it without hesitation to the man's right eye.

He closed his eyes just moments before the tip touched, and the blade bit into the lid. "I'll talk."

Parker moved back an inch. "Then talk."

"I pass on things to some o' the lords." He tried to pull himself together, to stay coherent. "Small things coming from France or the Netherlands."

"What things?"

"Little wooden boxes sometimes. Heavy coins."

"You've looked in the boxes." Parker did not make it a question.

"Aye. Screwed open the coins too. Some were made in haste, and I could see the join."

"What was in them?"

"Letters. And I can't read, 'afore you ask. I don't know what they said."

"And you are doing this for . . . ?"

"Never met him." His voice strengthened. "One night he come up behind me on me way home from the tavern.

Thought I was done for. Knife at me throat, an' all. Says a sailor will give me something to pass on later that day."

"I certainly hope the money was good." Parker swiped the drop of blood from the man's eyelid off the tip of his knife. "And that you enjoyed it while you could. You've been passing treasonous letters from Richard de la Pole to his supporters against the King, and I don't think they care much for that in the Tower."

All the blood drained from the attacker's face. His throat worked, trying to swallow. "I swear, I *swear*, I didn't know." He began shivering again.

"You know that matters not at all." Parker made to stand, and with his good arm, the man grabbed him.

"Please. I've been honest. I'll tell you everything. Everything, I swear it."

"I'm too weary. You are the third to attack me and mine this day alone. The sixth since I met that ship in Deal. I'll let the Tower do the work for me this time." Parker pried the man's fingers from his arm.

"Please." He was crying, heaving air into his lungs. "Do you think them what picked up those letters aren't to do with the Tower? With the King? If they find out I'm there, I won't last five minutes."

Parker looked at him, considering. "You can identify them?"

The man painfully tapped his head. "I got a good eye for faces. I c'n remember faces and the days we met."

"We draw up a list." Parker crouched down again. "Dates, times, the ship you received each message from, and the name of the courtier you handed it to."

He nodded eagerly.

"What is your name?" Parker stood.

"Marcus, m'lord."

"I'll send the healer out to you, Marcus. When she has finished dealing with the victims of your handiwork."

Marcus winced. "Your pardon, m'lord—"

"Stop." Parker's voice was harsh. "You attacked two small boys and a woman for money. You cannot be sorrier than I." He began walking toward the door, then turned back. "If you lie to me just once, if you try to run, if you steer me wrong—by God, you'll be begging me to hand you to the Tower." He held Marcus's gaze, saw the stricken look in his eyes, and delivered his final warning. "I am at the end of my patience, with no mercy left in me."

As he walked into the yard, he looked toward the lane and wondered wearily who would be trying to breach his home next.

Defensive moves were no longer enough. It was time to start moving his own pieces in this mysterious and deadly game of chess, before someone removed his queen—a painter from Ghent who had somehow touched his soul.

———

H arvey's wife."

Susanna opened her eyes as Parker sank wearily down next to her before the study fire. She struggled to shake off her exhaustion. At last the house was quiet. The body in the stable had been taken away. The other attacker had been taken to Father Haden, lest someone try to silence him before he could fulfill his promise to Parker, and Mistress Greene and the boys seemed to be resting easily.

"You think all this is to stop me giving Harvey's message to his wife?" They had both thought it, just before Mistress Greene had cried out, but Susanna had since dismissed the notion.

"If it was for her. What exactly did Harvey say?" Parker's eyes seemed feverish in the firelight, the contours of his face stark.

"He gave me the message for the King, said he knew how the messages were getting through. Then he stopped suddenly and stared over my shoulder, his eyes filled with horror." Susanna curled her fingers around her wrist where Harvey had grasped her, so weak he could barely hold on. "Then he said: 'My wife. I have provided for my wife's future. She holds my secrets.'"

"Did you look over your shoulder?" Parker asked.

Susanna shook her head. "I wanted to, but I was afraid. I knew there could be no one behind me, but the way Harvey looked, so focused, it felt as if Death truly could be standing at my back. I was too much a coward to look."

"It was good that you did not."

The way Parker spoke, so hard and flat, made her frown. "You think someone *was* behind me?"

He nodded. "Someone Harvey knew."

"He was telling them something. Warning them his wife had a secret hidden, that they could not kill her without risking discovery." Susanna leaned forward and grabbed Parker's arm in excitement. "We must go to her."

He nodded, but she could see his energy had been leached out by the long day. "Tomorrow is soon enough. I need rest."

"Did you get Maggie to look at you?" Susanna recalled the beating he had taken in the stable, and compressed her lips as he shook his head.

"No time, and all I have is bruises."

"Are you sure?"

He gave her a lopsided smile, leaning back against his chair. "Are you offering to play the healer, Mistress Horenbout?"

Susanna felt her face flush, and her voice was gone for a moment. There was a longing in his eyes, a true invitation behind the dry humor. "I . . ."

He began to close her off, his wall coming down again, and she shoved her shyness aside.

"Yes."

He focused on her, and his eyes glittered in the firelight.

"I will get warm water from the kitchen." Her words tripped over themselves, but she rose as calmly as she could. "This room is the warmest, so you can start taking off your doublet, if you are able."

His face was serious, his brows drawn together. "I was not talking only of seeing to my wounds—"

"I know what you were talking about." Susanna walked to the door, then turned to look at him.

Parker grinned back at her. "As long as we're in accord."

12

The Chiefe Conditions and Qualities in a Courtier: His
love towarde women, not to be sensuall or fleshlie,
but honest and godly, and more ruled with reason,
then appetyte: and to love better the beawtye of the
minde, then of the bodie.

*Of the Chief Conditions and Qualityes in a Waytyng
Gentylwoman:* Not to be lyghte of creditt that she is
beloved, though a man commune familierlye with
her of love.

He was too tired for this sweet torture. And too stiff.

Parker winced as Susanna applied salve to an open
cut on his arm, where he'd been sliced open by his own shovel
in one of his many rolls on the stable floor with Marcus.

He was getting old.

He needed to start thinking instead of fighting, but it
wasn't as if he'd had any choice.

Her fingers brushed his shoulder, and then she placed a
warm, wet cloth over the deep purple bruise there. The solu-
tion she'd dipped the cloth in had a pungent smell, but he
could feel his muscles relax as the heat did its work.

Despite being half-naked in a room alone with Susanna

Horenbout, he would not be doing what he'd wanted to since the moment he saw her.

Ravishing her.

Just the thought of it made him smile.

"I would have my way with you—you know that, don't you?"

He saw a smile dance on her lips and then disappear. "I know."

"And as you do not run, the thought is obviously not repugnant to you?"

Her hands stilled. "No."

"Perhaps you should run." The words stuck in his throat.

Her hands gripped him just tight enough to make him wince. "Perhaps I should. But I won't."

"And your blacksmith?" Ever since Susanna had mentioned him, Parker had felt the man's presence like a stone in his boot.

She started sponging his back again. "I am an artist, Parker. I do not cook, I do not clean. I work long hours on commissions my father receives from lords and royalty throughout Europe. I would make a poor wife."

Parker waited, wanting to hear everything before he spoke.

"But I am no nun. I want to experience the pleasures of the bed. I thought my father—I thought he would understand that. See me as he sees my brother. But he took very badly to my clumsy attempts at seducing the blacksmith who works with him on some of his larger commissions."

"Were you successful? In your seduction?" Parker made his

voice level, but he could feel the tension in her fingers as she stopped sponging.

"What if I was?"

"I will not lie and say it matters not to me, but it will change nothing between us."

She made a helpless twitch of frustration. "I was not successful." She sighed. He heard the regret in it and felt a stir of chagrin. "So close we were, and my father . . ." She squeezed out the cloth absently, as if thinking back to the moment before her father caught her in her blacksmith's arms.

Something new reared within him. He'd felt possessive of her since the first crossbow bolt embedded itself in the door above her shoulder. But now he wanted to act. To make sure the world could see what he already knew. What she needed to know herself.

That she was his.

He rose, quicker than she was expecting, put his hands on her, and jerked her hips to his.

She gave a quick, nervous swallow, and tried to pull back. He held her in place.

"I am in no state tonight to do anything about my desires for you, my lady. But next time you remember a kiss, I would prefer it to be mine."

He bent his head to hers and touched her softly, holding himself in check, falling slowly, gradually into a thing that took on a life of its own.

He was deaf, suddenly, and blind, and his only impressions were of her sweet rosemary scent and the softness of her lips.

She made a noise, a gasp, and he realized he had backed her into his desk, that she was about to fall over it.

As carefully as he could, he stepped back.

She looked at him, wild-eyed, her breath coming in pants. She lifted a shaking hand to her mouth.

As he limped slowly from the room, he decided he had achieved his aim. She would not think of her blacksmith again.

———

"You were there when my husband died?"

Mistress Harvey looked at Susanna uncertainly. She seemed confused, half-dazed, and Susanna could see they had roused the woman from her bed, although the morning was almost halfway gone.

"Yes, I was on the same ship as he, and tried to give him some relief as he lay dying. He entrusted a last message for you to me."

Mistress Harvey made a sound of distress, enough to divert Parker's gaze from his post at the window into the plushly decorated room, but he swung immediately back to the street, watchful and ready.

Despite her exhaustion, or perhaps because of it, Susanna's mind drifted back to last night. He had looked just as dangerous then, but his intense focus had been on her. On wanting her.

When he was alone with her, Parker's smile reached all the way up to his eyes.

She shivered.

"What was the message?" Mistress Harvey whispered. She was pale, pinched. Afraid.

Embarrassed at her wandering mind, Susanna straightened. "He said he'd provided for your future. That you held his secrets."

Mistress Harvey gave a cry, and Susanna saw Parker frown.

"Madam." His voice was harsh and impatient. "Since attending to your husband in his last hours, Mistress Horenbout has been attacked five times. The matter involves the King, and as his courtier, I am bound to see this to a resolution."

The widow began to weep.

"Do you know anything of this?" Susanna reached out a tentative hand and placed it on her heaving shoulder.

"I begged my husband, begged him over and over through the years, to cease his prying. I told him no good would ever come of stealing secrets." She lifted a trembling hand to wipe her eyes.

"What secret did he entrust to you?" Parker's voice was softer now that he saw she would cooperate.

Mistress Harvey pursed her lips. "I didn't want to know it. So I kept it folded, as he gave it to me. It has been a burden to me since the moment it lay in my hand."

She went to a small desk set against a wall and slipped a hand behind one of the legs. With a snick, a small drawer slid out, and Mistress Harvey withdrew a letter from it with fumbling fingers.

Parker took the folded parchment she held out and as he

read it, his expression grew . . . frightening. Cold, controlled. Susanna believed him capable of almost anything in that moment.

"Where did your husband get this?" Parker hadn't moved an inch from the window, but it was as if he'd stepped toe-to-toe with Mistress Harvey. As if he loomed over her.

She trembled. "I know not. I can tell you when he came by the secret, but that is all I know. As soon as he told me it concerned the King, I wanted no part of it. But he said it was our safeguard. Someone he feared would not move against us while we had the letter."

Susanna could see the stark fear on her face, and suddenly knew Mistress Harvey did not speak true. She did know the secret. Either she had looked, or she'd known since the beginning.

Parker said nothing for a moment, then he slipped the parchment into his money pouch. "Tell me all you know."

"He attended a merchants' guild meeting a year ago. He came back excited, spent the next day out of the house. When he returned that evening, he was afraid. Nervous. As if he regretted hunting down the rumor he'd heard. Now that he had the truth, he didn't want it."

"Common sense intervened, then." Parker's tone was dry, but Susanna could see he held himself in check with iron will. Whatever was on that paper had made something clear to him, and it had shaken the ground beneath him. He seemed to vibrate with tension.

"We must go. I don't need to ask you to keep this quiet, do

I?" He held Mistress Harvey's gaze, and Susanna saw her go paler still.

"No, sir. You need not."

He nodded, taking hold of Susanna's arm and pulling her along in his wake.

As they stepped outside, the front door was slammed hard and fast behind them, making her start in surprise.

"Why was she lying?" She pitched her voice low.

Parker gave her a considering look.

"She is lying because she knows the King will kill anyone who knows the secret on this paper. Swearing she doesn't know is her only chance of survival."

"How do we know this secret is even true?"

Parker quirked his lip. "Under normal circumstances, we wouldn't."

Susanna drew her cloak around her as they approached Parker's cart. "But in this case?"

"In this case, I know this secret is true because I already knew it."

"And yet here you are, alive." Susanna smiled, but Parker did not smile with her.

"Until the moment I read that paper, I thought I was the only one left alive, save two, who did know it."

Susanna swallowed the lump that formed in her throat. "Who are the other two?"

"The King himself and his brother-in-law, Charles Brandon, the Duke of Suffolk." Parker lifted her up onto the cart, then untied the reins.

"So how did Harvey discover it?"

"There is only one way. Either the King or Suffolk has talked. And we can only hope to God it was Suffolk."

"And if it was the King?" Susanna moved over on the driving bench, and Parker joined her. He flicked the reins.

"Then we are dead."

13

The Chiefe Conditions and Qualities in a Courtier:
Not to be ill tunged, especiallie against his betters.

Of the Chief Conditions and Qualityes in a Waytyng Gentylwoman: Not to make wise to knowe the thing that she knoweth not, but with sobernesse gete her estimation with that she knoweth.

W hat is the secret?"

Parker turned his attention from the rutted road to look at Susanna's serious face. "It's safer if you don't know."

"Whoever is behind these attacks thinks I know anyway."

Frustration rose in him at the truth of her words. "It could be they thought Harvey had told you of the letter, not realizing his message for you had nothing to do with the secret he kept with his wife."

He wondered again who the bastard was, although he had his suspicions.

"Am I not damned either way, then? At least knowing the secret, I may be of some use to you. Some help."

Parker wasn't sure when someone had last offered to help him.

"Parker?" A frown creased her brow, and he had to hold himself back from touching her.

There were dark circles under her eyes and her skin was pale, almost translucent. Her eyes held a spark, though. Tired but determined.

If he could not trust her with the truth, he could not trust anyone. And for a long time, he'd thought trusting no one was the only wise thing he could do.

But he was so tired of the cold loneliness of the last few years. So tired of looking at each hand extended in friendship with suspicion.

He wanted the safe haven he could see in her smile.

"I cannot tell you here. Let us get home." He urged the cart horse forward, bracing an arm around Susanna as they hit a deep pothole and the cart lurched over it.

He felt too exposed on the street. He was only one man, and whoever wished to silence them had many at his disposal.

Given the new information Mistress Harvey had provided, they could be under attack from two fronts. Harvey had been playing two dangerous games.

But Parker had a surprise up his sleeve: the plan he'd put into place with Peter Jack early yesterday morning.

Unusual though it might be, he had his own army to call in.

The house was quiet. Susanna had been dismayed to find Mistress Greene in the kitchen that morning, but the housekeeper had promised to lie down if she needed to.

Susanna had watched her chop vegetables, look in on the boys, and make bread. She moved slowly, but each movement was a deliberate reclamation of her territory. She gathered up the rushes before the fireplace, stained dark with her blood, and threw them into the fire. Then she slapped her hands together as if ridding them of dust, and turned her back on the flames.

Tears had prickled behind Susanna's eyes at the house-keeper's determination and bravery. To cover her weakness, she'd busied herself, putting on a kettle to boil, sweeping the floor, all in silence. She felt the same quiet companionship with Mistress Greene that she'd had with her mother, completing small tasks together in the kitchen.

Now, with the house so still, they looked in at the kitchen, and Susanna thought Parker always would, until the end of his days. He would never enter his house again without checking the well-being of each person in it.

Mistress Greene slept in the big chair by the kitchen fire, still pale and hollow-eyed, and a quick look at the boys showed they slept too, empty soup bowls sitting on the small table between their narrow beds.

Eric looked much better, his color back; but Peter Jack's face was a mess of cuts and bruises, smeared green with the unguent Maggie had left for them to apply. He stirred as they backed out of the room and opened his right eye, his left swollen shut.

"All well?" he croaked, his voice rough. Marcus had hit him across the throat, and Maggie had said it could take a week for his voice to recover.

"Shhh." Susanna stepped forward and crouched beside him. "All is well. Parker and I will be in his study if you need us. Go back to sleep."

Peter Jack shook his head. "I'm tired o' sleeping."

"Give us a few minutes, then," Parker told him, coming up behind her. "There is something I must tell Mistress Horenbout in private, but then you are welcome to join us."

"Need the privy, anyway."

Susanna helped him to sit up, and was enveloped in the strong herbal scent of the unguent. He shook his head at her offered hand and struggled to his feet on his own.

He hobbled behind them into the kitchen and started for the back door.

She watched him make his slow, painful way across the floor, then hold the wall, teetering as he slipped his feet into his outdoor boots. For the first time since she'd met him, he looked closer to the child he was than the young man he would become. She felt a fresh wave of anger at Marcus and the man who had sent him. Her breath caught in her throat and stuttered out as she exhaled, fists clenched.

"Even with the beatin', this is still the best me 'n' Eric ever had it." Peter Jack watched her, his right eye steady and clear, making the swollen red and purple of the left even more shocking.

"And, tell the truth, I'm glad we got into the thick. I was the one tryin' to kill you two nights ago. I feel like I earned me right to stay now. I fought for you, and I will again, mistress."

Tears, sharp as rose thorns against the backs of her eyes, threatened and then spilled out.

She could not answer him. If she did, she would sob. She had to breathe in deeply to stop herself as it was. He seemed to understand, because when she blinked her eyes clear, the door was closing behind him and he was gone.

She composed herself and turned to find Parker staring at her from the doorway.

"You inspire loyalty, my lady." His eyes held some emotion that seized her throat and grabbed at her heart.

"No more than you." Her voice trembled.

"Nay. I inspire fear. Or envy. But seldom loyalty."

"You inspire it in me." The way he was leaning against the door, his eyes intense in his lean face, his posture alert and poised, inspired more than loyalty. Her hand reached for her satchel, closed around air, and she remembered it was in her room. She would paint him just like this as soon as she could. She tried to imprint the picture he made in her memory.

"You honor me." As he straightened up, his expression was unreadable.

She felt a tingle at her nape. John Parker was beyond anything she'd dealt with before. A life spent in her father's atelier had not prepared her for him.

"Let us talk before Peter Jack returns from the privy." He gestured down the passageway and she followed him, her mind no longer on the secret. She wanted nothing more than a day of quiet, her paints, and enough light to paint by. And the company of her model.

"Are you sure you wish to know this?" Parker sat again in the right-hand chair, leaving her the left. They were beginning to have their own chairs by the fire, little rituals of comfort and accommodation. Some sort of shared life.

Susanna paused. It was on the tip of her tongue to tell him she had changed her mind, she did not want to hear the secret. But not hearing it would make none of this go away.

"I wish only for an end to this, and hearing the secret may help us. It certainly cannot harm us."

"It could harm you, if the Tower got hold of you." His voice was grim.

"If the Tower called for me in this matter, I would be harmed whether I know the secret or not. And the more I swore I didn't know, the more harm would befall me."

He nodded tersely in agreement, then turned to face the fire.

"I was a dock rat of gentle birth. The oldest son of a second son. My father was cast out from his family because of a disagreement with his father, and when he died, my younger brother and I worked the docks to help my mother put food on the table."

Susanna tried to picture him as he had been, as ragged and sharp as Peter Jack.

"One day I was working at unloading a shipment of lace from France, and a Frenchman off the ship asked me the way to the palace. The King was in Westminster in those days, just a few short years after he'd been crowned."

Parker crossed his arms and leaned back in his chair. "The Frenchman was a mercenary, by the look of him. Hard, cruel. He was the type to rob bodies on the battlefield. I didn't know what he was up to, and not wanting trouble, I told him the way."

Susanna watched as Parker turned his thumbs around and around each other, seeming to be in another place. "Go on."

He started, and flashed her a rueful look. "That night I was skulking around one of the taverns, hoping for some food from the kitchens, and I saw him returning to his ship. As he walked into the deep shadow of a warehouse, he was set upon by two men."

Parker sat straighter. "I was torn. It was two against one, yet I had no liking for the man. I went forward with no clear idea what action I would take. Suddenly two other men leaped into the fray, on the mercenary's side. It seemed to me they must have been following him on his orders, in case he was set upon. It was a deeper game than I'd first thought."

"What happened?" Susanna realized she'd lowered her voice.

"I continued to approach, though my instincts told me to walk away. I heard a shout from one of the two who had first set upon the Frenchman, and it was as if my blood turned to winter rain."

He shook his head, and it seemed to Susanna he was reliving his disbelief at another's stupidity. "It was a particular battle cry often used at the royal jousting tournaments, and in the days when my father was alive I had been to more than a few. I knew immediately whose call it was."

"Whose?" Susanna asked.

"The King's. The King of England and a courtier were attacking the Frenchman on the docks."

Susanna gasped. "Why would he be so bold?"

"So careless, you mean?" Parker raised his eyebrows. "He often went out in disguise to mingle with the commoners, I discovered afterward. But this time it was in deadly earnest. He'd been approached by the Frenchman at court as he went out to hunt earlier that day, and it was clear the mercenary had a letter Henry could not allow to be made public. He decided to get it back himself, with only Brandon at his side, to keep all knowledge of it secret from others at court."

"What did you do?" Susanna asked.

"What could I do?" Parker sounded resigned. "I leaped in on the King's behalf, although I had no weapon but the knife I always carried." He smiled faintly. "The King and Brandon were pleased to have me, as they were used to courtly games of mock battle and set rules of engagement—not the street fighting of a mercenary and his dockhand helpers.

"With my help, the King managed to take the Frenchman down and cut his purse from his belt. As soon as he had it in hand, Brandon grabbed him, and both the King and I noticed then what only Brandon had seen: that a crowd had drifted over from the taverns to watch the fight."

Again, Parker shook his head. "The King·was in even graver danger. Danger of his life, and danger of discovery. Brandon urged him away, and they ran off."

"Leaving you to face the crowd?" Shock made her voice tremble.

"It was my duty to keep the men the Frenchman had hired away from the King. And it helped that they were uncertain what to do—their paymaster was dead or injured, and some of the fight had gone out of them. They carried on because they thought they could take me and win. But I had a stroke of fortune. One of the men in the crowd recognized me and called out my name. Thinking the balance of numbers was about to turn against them, they ran off."

"Were you hurt?"

"A cut on my arm, some bruises." Parker waved the question off as of no concern. "I knelt at the Frenchman's side, and could feel there was faint life in him. He was bleeding and unconscious. I checked his coat and his shirt to see if there was any way to identify him, and deep inside his cloak, cleverly hidden in the lining, was a deep pocket with a letter in it."

"The letter the King was looking for?"

"Aye." Parker steepled his fingers. "The mercenary had taken the letter out of his pouch when he'd approached the King earlier, but must have decided it wasn't safe enough there."

"So now you had the letter." Susanna wondered what the King had done when he'd realized the letter was not in the pouch he'd risked his life and reputation to get.

"I had the letter," Parker agreed. "And from what I could see, that was as good as having a price on my head."

14

The Chiefe Conditions and Qualities in a Courtier: To play upon the Vyole, and all other instruments with freates.

Of the Chief Conditions and Qualityes in a Waytyng Gentylwoman: To be seene in the most necessarie languages.

What was written in that letter?" Susanna hugged her arms close to stop herself trembling. Parker hesitated, as if he truly believed he should not tell her this.

"The year before old King Henry died, he locked our present King away for many months. The Prince was not allowed to speak unless spoken to. He took his lessons mostly from his father, and did not speak to any tutors brought in. They lectured him, and he listened in silence. He could speak to no other courtiers, and if he wished to go outside, he had to leave by a side door into the park. He took all his meals in his room, and on one occasion the King almost killed him, beating him until his courtiers intervened."

"What happened?" Susanna realized she was leaning forward, her body tense.

"No one knew. Some said that with his oldest son dead, the King was taking pains to protect his only remaining heir. Some said he was keeping the prince close, and teaching him the ways of kingship."

"But the truth of it was . . . ?"

"The truth of it was that the prince had become obsessed with Cesare Borgia. Borgia had just been killed in battle in Navarre, fighting against the French King at his brother-in-law's side. His story was one of daring, courage, and bravery. He was larger than life, irresistible to the young Prince."

"What harm was there in that?"

Parker sighed, rubbed his forehead. "There would have been none, had the Prince not decided he would like a similar life. He was close to his brother Arthur's widow, now our Queen, and he wrote to her father, Ferdinand of Spain, asking for a small army and a cause to fight against the French on the Continent."

Susanna gasped at the implications. "He did not ask his father's permission?"

"Nay. You can only imagine what the King would have said to that. The Prince planned to sneak away with the help of his closest friend, Charles Brandon, now Duke of Suffolk."

There was a creak at the door, and Parker was on his feet, knife in hand, before Susanna had even turned to look.

It was Peter Jack.

"Wait a moment in the kitchen, please. I will call you

when we are ready." Parker relaxed his stance but remained standing as Peter Jack limped away down the passage. It was a testament to the story's grip that neither had heard his approach.

"A messenger handed Henry's missive to the old King before it was sent, and his rage was boundless. He came to blows with the Prince. He believed that Ferdinand would have taken the Prince's defiance and poor sense as a mark against the whole royal family. He put the Prince under constant watch."

"How did you discover all this?"

"It so happened there was another missive—one that was never intercepted. The Prince had sent it to Borgia's brother-in-law, D'Albret, declaring his admiration for Borgia and his contempt for the Pope, the French King, and even the Spanish, who had imprisoned Borgia for two years before he escaped."

"The letter was truly insulting?" Susanna was finally beginning to see the reason for the desperation behind the attacks. The Pope, the French King, and the Spanish King were powerful people to insult.

"All three had stuck a knife in Borgia's back." Parker spoke not with contempt, exactly, but with an edge to his tone. She knew that, even as a young man, he would not have idolized anyone to the extent that Henry had idolized Borgia. Parker lived by his own rules; while she was sure he held some men in respect, he would never follow their path. He would always forge his own.

Parker turned from the door and paced toward the fire. "Somehow, that letter fell out of D'Albret's hands and into those of a Frenchman who found passage to London as a sailor."

"The mercenary?"

"Aye. After I found the letter, I went to find Maggie to see to the Frenchman's wounds. When we returned, he had bled to death."

"What did he want for the letter? Money?"

"I can only assume he thought it would make him his fortune."

"And now you held something you could not keep." Susanna wondered what she would have done in Parker's place. Destroyed it, most likely.

Parker returned to his chair, his body turned toward her.

"I begged a favor. Since my father's death, it had been a point of pride for my brother and me not to beg for help. But my father's family had land and was well-regarded, and my father had studied with some who were in elevated positions. I called on one of them, and convinced him to get me before the King."

"Did he recognize you? From the night you helped him?"

Parker shook his head, a small smile lifting the corners of his mouth. "But when I mentioned the fight, I suddenly had his full attention and the private audience I'd requested. I presented him with the letter and told him all I knew. Threw myself on his mercy."

Susanna recalled the King's cold eyes when he'd realized she knew something dangerous to him, and shivered. "What did he do?"

Parker took her hand, as if reading her mind. "He was grateful. And for some reason, he saw something in me. He liked the way I'd fought. Liked that I'd joined him in the fray unasked. Either that, or he had a mind to keep his potential enemies close." Parker gave a laugh. "He offered me a position within the Privy Chamber. He said my coming to him with the letter and offering it up with no request for a boon spoke to my character."

Parker's eyes looked past her out the darkening window, his hold on her hand firm. "I think he must have ordered someone to look into my background, because shortly thereafter I learned that my father's older brother and all his family had died of the sweating sickness, and as my father's eldest son, I was the heir."

"You did not know of your uncle's death?" Susanna felt a frisson of shock.

"He was not overpleased when my mother appealed to him for help upon my father's death, and my brother and I resolved to make a living without him. Once allied to the King, overnight I found myself with land holdings in Fulham, and soon after that I inherited a distant cousin's property in Hertfordshire."

"And your brother?" Susanna was intrigued. She had not thought Parker had any family.

"He and his wife and my mother live on my estates in Hertfordshire. My brother manages the property for me." His thumb began to stroke the top of her hand, back and forth.

Susanna relaxed into her chair. Parker could excite her

with nothing more than a look, but this gentle stroking was calming. Soothing and protective. "These attacks on us are to stop us from talking of the letter?"

"I don't know." Parker's eyes glittered with frustration. "There is more than one plot in play here. The letter is one, de la Pole's connivance against the King another. Both contain more treachery than I can believe." He rubbed his brow. "It could be that Brandon wishes to silence us, because he spoke out of turn to Harvey or to one of Harvey's informants. With either plot, disloyalty to the King takes on a new significance."

Parker released her hand, rose, and walked to the door. "The real mystery is the letter itself. I saw it destroyed with my own eyes by the King, the afternoon I gave it to him. He threw it in the fire." Parker lifted his money purse, his mouth a grim line. "And yet, despite the evidence of my own eyes, once more I find it in my possession."

―――――――――

M ay I see it?"
Susanna held out her hand, and Parker hesitated. Wasn't he risking her enough as it was, just telling her his secrets?

"I am an illuminator, Parker. Paper, letters, books—they are my lifeblood." Her hand held steady, and he dropped the letter into her palm.

He paced, agitated, as she smoothed it open, then looked at it for what felt like long minutes.

"This is not the original letter, I think." Susanna flicked a finger against the paper.

"It was long ago that I read it, but the wording sounds the same." Parker came to stand at her shoulder, looking more closely at the paper.

"This is a draft, perhaps. The wording is uncertain; mistakes have been made." Susanna pointed to two words that had been heavily blotted out, and the lines scored through others. "There is no seal on this either." She rubbed the paper between finger and thumb. "The paper is high-quality, but perhaps the King never uses less expensive paper for his drafts?"

Parker laughed. "No. Probably not." He thought the implications through for a moment, and felt a slight easing of the tension that had gripped him since Mistress Harvey had handed him the letter.

"What is it?"

It startled him that she could feel the change in him without his saying a word.

"This means Brandon might not be behind this after all. A clerk, a page boy, anyone could have stolen the draft. It widens our list of suspects."

A huge weight lifted from him. Pointing a finger at Brandon would have tested his friendship and service to the King to its limits.

Susanna turned her head to look up at him, and he was struck dumb for a moment. In the fire's glow, she was all hazel eyes and cream skin, the luster of her hair and the clarity of her gaze almost shocking in their purity. "This is a good thing?"

He barely registered her question, until he saw the thin, dark line where Gripper's knife had cut under her chin. It focused him despite the heat of her body, inches from his own.

"This is the best news possible." Had he falsely accused Brandon, he would have been buried alive.

Susanna leaned into him, giving support, not taking it. His arms began to lift to draw her closer, then froze as he saw Peter Jack in the doorway, a cheeky grin on his bruised face.

"Are ye ready for me?"

Despite himself, Parker grinned back. He'd like to close that door and forget everything in Susanna's touch and heat. But that luxury would have to wait.

"Aye. Sit yourself down." He stepped back and pulled his chair closer to the fire for Peter Jack. "We need to call in our troops."

Peter Jack sat, wincing like an old man.

"Troops?" Susanna looked between them, curious.

"My lads," Peter Jack explained. "We put them to work."

"I sent one to keep an eye on the archer we left at Blackfriars," Parker said. "One is watching Father Haden's, and the rest have become my eyes and ears on the street."

"When did you do all this?" Susanna sounded stunned.

"Yesterday morning, before you were attacked in the yard," Peter Jack answered. "Before the war really got going."

"A lifetime ago." Susanna sank back into her chair.

"Aye. Feels like it to me too." Peter Jack stretched thin legs out toward the leaping flames.

"Get used to it." Parker made sure they were both looking at him before he continued. "Things are going to get worse."

15

The Chiefe Conditions and Qualities in a Courtier: To
speake alwaies of matters likely, least he be counted
a lyer in reporting of wonders and straunge miracles.

*Of the Chief Conditions and Qualityes in a Waytyng
Gentylwoman:* To take the lovynge communication
of a sober Gentylman in an other signifycatyon,
seeking to straye from that pourpose.

A more ragtag, tattered unit he had never seen. The boys
were painfully thin and feral, and their clothes were
filthy. They needed to be one level up, Parker thought. Ap-
prentices or messengers. They must become part of the crowd
of rascal boys who plagued the palace.

They stood huddled in his courtyard, shivering, and he remembered just how sharply the damp winter air could bite
through a rough wool vest.

"Come with me," he told them, and saw the collective
look of surprise as they realized he meant them to follow him
indoors.

That was the difference between them and the boy he had
been. He had been used to entering fine houses. And he now

owned some of the ones he'd visited. These boys had only ever known the gutter.

"We're none too clean, sir." The boy who spoke was Harry, the de facto leader of the group now that Peter Jack had moved on to greener pastures.

"That is why you need to come inside. You need a wash and better clothes if you're to be of any use to me."

Parker continued up the back steps, aware of the horrified silence behind him.

"Wash?" It was one of the younger ones. If Parker was any judge, the only water he'd ever had on him was from standing in the rain.

"And eat."

Parker waited a beat, heard them start up the stairs after him.

In the kitchen, his strange new family was at the table. Somehow Susanna had united them, unlikely though they were.

She stood as he entered, and took in the six ragamuffins behind him.

There was a shout of joy from Eric, and he leaped from his chair to wrestle with the lads as they crowded in. He looked completely recovered.

Peter Jack hauled himself up as well, and the boys stopped their horseplay as soon as they noticed him. It was the quiet of respect.

"Been in a fight?" Harry asked.

"Aye." Peter Jack said nothing more, but he drew himself up straighter.

"He was helping Master Parker protect me," Susanna said, and reached out a hand to touch Peter Jack's shoulder. He ducked away, but not before Parker saw the flash of pride in his eyes.

"Right, lads. You need food and a bath." Mistress Greene rose from the table, and the boys' eyes widened at the sight of her. With the bandage around her head, the bruising on her left cheek already green and purple, she looked formidable.

She lifted a bucket of water from beside the stove and poured it into a large kettle over the fire.

"Don't ye want our report first?" Harry sidled out of her reach.

"Why don't you have a bite while you talk?" Mistress Greene bent to take bowls from a cupboard, set them on the table, and began ladling meaty broth to the brim.

"Couple o' Lord Mucks, ain't ya?" Harry said around a mouthful to Peter Jack and Eric. He hadn't even waited to sit.

"You could be too, Harry. If you and the boys have a bath, disguise yourselves for me, and make yourselves useful, we could come to some arrangement." Parker closed the back door and leaned against it. "I'll deal fairly with you."

Harry eyed him nervously, and Parker realized he was blocking their only escape. He straightened from the door-jamb and moved to the fire, leaving the way out clear.

"You'll need to come up with the goods for the job we just done," Harry told him, a little more relaxed.

Parker nodded, pulled out his money pouch, and counted out the sum they'd agreed on earlier.

The other lads elbowed each other gleefully at the sight of the coins, but Harry kept a straight face. It must have cost him, but he was determined to be all business.

"First up, what about Kinnock?" Peter Jack leaned forward on his elbows, his eyes sharp on Harry's face.

"Kinnock?" Susanna frowned.

"One o' the lads," Eric explained to her. "Least, he *was*. Seems he's the one set Peter Jack on ya. Took the money and left us all high and dry."

Peter Jack's face hardened, and Parker felt a part of him tighten in understanding. The pain of betrayal by someone you trusted. He was sorry Peter Jack had to know that so young.

But someone had already betrayed him, all of them, for them to be living under a riverside quay in winter.

Harry lifted his bowl and gulped down the last of his broth. He started in surprise as Mistress Greene handed him a hunk of bread to wipe the bowl clean. He swallowed it in a single bite. "Kinnock's nowheres to be seen. I went to all the places I could think of. He's gone."

"You know all his hidey-holes?" Parker asked.

"Thought I knew *him*. Now . . ." Harry shrugged, trying for nonchalance and almost carrying it off. Another one Kinnock had hurt by selling his crew down the river.

"And the other jobs?" Parker crossed his arms over his chest.

"The archer at Blackfriars is dead." The boy who spoke up looked about seven years old. He spoke of death without a hitch in his voice.

"Murdered?" Susanna asked sharply, and Parker recalled it was at her insistence they had saved the archer at all.

The boy shook his head. "That monk you told me to give the message to, he said his blood got poisoned. They couldn't save him."

"Was anyone hovering there? Anyone looking for a chance to get to him?" Parker wished he could have been there himself.

"One." The boy nodded. "Said as he were there to speak to a monk, but he was lying."

Parker didn't ask him how he knew; these boys could spot a liar at fifty paces. They wouldn't be alive long on the streets otherwise.

"You followed him?" It's what Parker would have done. The boy nodded, and sat up straighter as Parker gave him a closer look. "What's your name?"

"Will, m'lord."

"Where did he go, Will?"

"Well . . ." Clearly uncomfortable, Will looked down at his empty bowl as if he could wish another helping into it. "He went across the bridge from the monastery into the palace, sir. They wouldn't let me in after him."

He shouldn't be surprised. Hadn't Marcus told him the men he'd dealt with were from the highest echelons? Any one of the courtiers could have sent a servant to finish off the archer—but there was only so much loyalty one could expect from a servant. If he knew who it was, perhaps he could get them to talk.

"Will, I am going to watch the palace later today. I want you with me, to see if you can point out this man."

Will nodded uncertainly. "I c'n try, sir."

"You are taking Marcus to watch the palace? To see if he recognizes any of the courtiers?" Susanna asked him.

"*We* are, yes." Parker stood. "Until this business is resolved, you go where I go, my lady."

Susanna's eyes widened. "But that means . . ." She was clearly unhappy.

"What?" Parker was at a loss.

"I'll have to sit in a carriage with that man."

"What man?" Will asked, leaning forward with interest.

"The one whose arm she nearly chopped off," Eric explained, pointing to the cleaver on the counter.

There was a moment of perfect silence.

"He'll be more worried'n you, most like," Will said, and bit down on a piece of bread.

Marcus's skin was the pale gray of dishwater, and he was sweating, his eyes feverish. It was clear he should not be out of his bed, but Susanna could summon no sympathy for him.

He'd forced her to maim him, to protect herself and the others, and she was as angry at him for that as for his attack on the boys and Mistress Greene. What she'd done to him would haunt her until she died, and she could not forgive him.

He leaned back against the plush seat inside the covered

carriage and glared at her with what little strength he had. Susanna looked him in the eye and felt his hatred like a physical blow. She drew in a little breath, and then narrowed her eyes.

They stared each other down for one beat, two; then Marcus closed his eyes. He lifted a trembling hand to his forehead and blotted the perspiration with a cloth.

"Never thought I'd see the inside o' one o' these," Will said in delight, oblivious to the atmosphere, and ran his hand over the black velvet seats. He fingered the curtains, parting them slightly, and Parker's hand shot out, his long fingers curling around Will's thin wrist.

Will grinned, slipped his wrist free, and began to admire his new clothes instead, holding out his arms and twisting them this way and that. He lifted his feet one at a time and gazed at his shoes. Though not new, they were well made, and likely the finest he'd ever had.

Susanna slipped out a piece of paper, grateful for the cunning windows cut in narrow rectangles around the roof of the carriage, giving those within natural light without compromising the anonymity the thick drapes provided.

She began to sketch Will, trying to capture the delight brimming from him at being warm and well clothed.

"Everyone seems right interested in us." Will turned to look out the window through the thin gap in the drapes, suddenly shy of being her focus.

Susanna had also noticed more than a few interested stares as men made their way to the main doors of the palace.

"They think the Queen or the Princess could be inside. This carriage is for their use." Parker edged the curtains a little farther apart. "Time to fulfill your end of the bargain." He tapped Marcus on the knee, and with an effort the dockhand opened his eyes and leaned forward.

"What if none I recognize come this way?" Marcus spoke with a tremble in his voice, and Susanna thought it was not all to do with his state of health. He feared Parker.

Parker smiled, and Susanna could see the wolf in it. "It would be useful to know who I can trust, as well as who I can't." He stared out the window again. "What about that one?"

He pointed to a short man, thin and pinched. He was dressed somberly but well and had a heavy gold collar of office over his cloak. He stared at the carriage for some moments, until Susanna was sure he would approach them. The way he set his lips and narrowed his eyes spoke of hardness and cruelty, and she felt a shudder of relief when at last he turned away.

Marcus shook his head. "Never seen him."

Parker looked after the man's narrow back and tapped his lips. "Norfolk would never have met you himself anyway. Were some who sought you out secretaries or men of affairs?"

Marcus nodded. "Some had ink-stained fingers. And their clothes weren't as fine."

"So you still won't know who you can trust," Susanna said, shading in the velvet seat behind Will on her sketch.

"Nothing I'm not used to." Parker's words were casual, his focus on those outside.

No wonder a cold wind howled behind his eyes. Parker was completely alone. Susanna lifted her charcoal from the paper and thought again of the painting she would do of him, leaning against the door frame of the kitchen in his fine blue doublet with saffron yellow embroidery on the collar. Big, wary, a look in his startling eyes that spoke of longing and resolve.

As if he knew she thought of him, he turned to her, and Susanna let herself fall into his bright blue gaze.

"There's one." Marcus's hiss made them both blink. He pointed at someone, tall and well-padded, with a crooked nose that looked too long in his face, coming down the palace steps.

"You're sure?" Parker's voice was clipped.

"I told you, I never forget a face," Marcus said.

"I can scarce credit—"

"There's the cove from the monastery." Will had insinuated himself between Marcus and Parker for a better look, and now he pointed to a stocky, compact man in a black doublet. Will's man seemed to be following the courtier Marcus had pointed out. He dodged behind a crowd leaving the palace as Marcus's man stopped and turned to look back. He stood for a moment, then shrugged and ran down the steps.

He moved well, Susanna noted, with the grace of a natural dancer. He carried himself well too, his shoulders straight and square despite the wobble in his belly.

She found herself liking the look of him, hoping he was not involved in this. She clamped down on the feeling.

Someone was responsible for the deaths that had dogged

her path since she'd left Ghent, and this was the closest they had come to finding out who.

She saw Parker's lips form a thin line. This man was known to him, she could see. And Parker liked him well.

Once again he would have to confront his enemy, but this time it would be with the bitter taste of betrayal on his tongue.

16

The Chiefe Conditions and Qualities in a Courtier: To be partly and amiable in countenance unto who so beehouldeth him.

Of the Chief Conditions and Qualityes in a Waytyng Gentylwoman: To be heedefull and remember that men may with lesse jeopardy show to be in love, then women.

Would this day never end? Parker stood with Susanna at the door of Francis Bryan's London rooms, and wondered what new twist this tale would take.

Bryan was one of the very few who amused the King in everything—at the jousts, in the hunt, and at play. He could joke, sing, dance, and fight—all the qualities His Majesty expected from those of his courtiers who didn't perform an actual service for him. But Bryan outdazzled most others.

Unlike himself, Parker thought with a wry twist of amusement. He had no singing voice, did not like dancing, and had seen enough violence to eschew playing at it in the jousts. The King seemed to like Parker all the more for this. He was an oddity, the exception that proved the rule. And of course, he was very, very useful.

With a brief glance at Susanna, Parker lifted the heavy knocker and smacked it down hard.

The crack summoned hurried footsteps, and the door was opened cautiously by a thin, nervous manservant.

Parker narrowed his eyes. So Bryan did have something to be nervous about?

"Tell Sir Francis that John Parker is here to see him." Parker stepped forward, Susanna on his arm, forcing the servant back.

The man darted a look at Susanna, as if expecting her name as well, but Parker merely stared at him, he sketched a hasty bow and hurried up a gloomy staircase.

"We are not even shown a seat?" Susanna asked quietly. "And he looked frightened enough to faint if you were to say boo."

"Aye. It looks as if Marcus spoke true. Bryan has something to hide, no question. But the servant's fright, the way Bryan looked on the palace steps . . ." Parker shook his head slowly. "If he is involved, it is not deeply. Whoever is behind this would be cooler. But Bryan knows something—"

"Ho, Parker." Bryan hailed them from the stairs as he made his way down, his face merry and bright. But the truth was in his eyes and the way his lips pursed.

"Bryan." Parker neither extended his hand nor bowed. A grave insult.

Bryan's eyes narrowed, then Parker saw him decide to let it

go. To ascribe it to the cold, or to ill-humor, anything other than what he feared: disrespect.

"I need to speak with you. In private." Parker kept his voice smooth.

Bryan tore his gaze away from Parker, his face a study in confusion and panic. He fixed his attention on Susanna.

"Did I not see you the other day, mistress? Waiting for a close council with the King? We were all most curious indeed as to your business with him." His voice was breathless.

"Your curiosity will not be satisfied, Bryan. And unless you would like me to discuss your treason against the King in your open hallway, you will invite us into one of your rooms. Now." Parker took a step forward, and Bryan all but flinched back.

The paragon of the jousts, with a sword arm second to none, cowered before him.

This was too deep a game for him, Parker decided in disgust. He wished for the quiet life of his Hertfordshire holdings. Even Fulham, despite its proximity to London, must be better than this.

"The King truly has sent you?" Bryan whispered.

Parker leaned closer. "I don't think you heard me, Bryan. I said *now*."

Something in Parker's imperious command at last stirred the man within Bryan's breast. He stood taller and did not flinch away. "Come with me, sir." His voice was cold and distant.

Perhaps it would have been better if he'd kept Bryan cowering, but Parker was glad the man had rediscovered his backbone. The world was topsy-turvy enough without Bryan acting like a milksop. It made Parker nervous.

He lost his temper when he was nervous.

And with Susanna Horenbout on his arm, he would prefer to remain in perfect control.

Bryan opened the door to a small, cold sitting room. A fire had been built in the hearth but not lit, and Bryan stared at it bemused, as if unsure what to do.

God save him from helpless nobles, Parker thought viciously. He let go of Susanna and stepped past Bryan, grabbing a small stick from the pile in the fireplace. He lit it from the candle on the table and within moments had the fire crackling.

"You are a man of many talents, Parker." Bryan spoke in a dry voice that teetered between contempt and admiration.

Parker was certain most of the King's courtiers felt the same way about him. He smiled. "The King certainly thinks so." He let that statement hang in the air, and motioned to Susanna to take a seat.

It was a testament to Bryan's distraction that he'd forgotten his manners to such an extent. As Susanna lowered herself into the plush velvet chair, Parker saw laughter and admiration in her eyes. He grinned back openly, and bent over her hand.

"Enough." Bryan's tone had gone from sardonic to nearly hysterical in moments. Parker turned slowly, an eyebrow raised. "Court your mysterious lady on your own time, Parker. Why are you here?"

"You know why I'm here, Bryan. When you began corresponding with de la Pole, you must have understood the risks." Parker leaned against Susanna's chair, his knife hand ready.

Bryan's face tried to remain outraged, and failed. "No," he whispered. "Who told you such a lie?"

"You in particular must know how easily some can be bought." Parker kept his voice even. "Perhaps when you were out in the streets of Paris with the King of France all those years ago, lobbing stones and eggs at the peasants, you were offered something you couldn't refuse? Did King Francis buy your loyalty that day?"

"That bastard Wolsey!" Bryan's throat worked and tendons stood out on his neck. "That he had spies watching me that day in Paris was bad enough. But to tell King Henry . . . to use that indiscretion as a way to remove me from the King . . ."

"Ah, come now, Bryan. Wolsey wasn't spying on you. You aren't important enough. It was the King of France who was of interest. And His Majesty invited you back to court soon after, didn't he? He finds you too merry and companionable to do without." Parker straightened up. "I wonder what he'll think of you now?"

The reality of that loss of patronage or, worse, the accusation of treason, hit Bryan full force. Parker watched his high color subside and an ashen white tint his skin.

"Parker," he whispered. "It is not what you think it is, I swear."

Parker perched on the arm of Susanna's chair. "It seldom is."

Although he could not be trusted, Susanna liked Francis Bryan. He would not lack for the company of women, nor the company of friends to drink with.

There was something about him. It was in the way he looked at a person, as if he was truly interested in them. If she were to paint him, she would have to find a way to capture the intensity of his gaze.

But Parker had disrupted his equilibrium. And he had done it like the master he was.

"The King is thinking of ending his marriage to the Queen." Bryan spoke quickly, as if saying it fast would make it sound better somehow. His eyes went nervously to Susanna. "I don't say this lightly, especially not with someone unknown to me in the room, but it's the truth."

Parker's gaze sharpened, but he did not look as surprised as Susanna was. He must have had an inkling of this himself.

"At present, it is but something he turns over in his mind. He needs a son, a legitimate son, and the Queen . . . well, her age, her fasting, and her kneeling in prayer in cold chapels for hours have made her courses erratic. There will be no more heirs from her, even if His Majesty slept regularly in her bed, which he does not."

Bryan looked from Susanna to Parker, and when they made no move or word to interrupt, he took a deep breath. "It seems he has no choice but to advance his illegitimate heir. And you can guess how the Queen will take her own daughter being usurped by His Majesty's bastard."

"It will not be pretty," Parker conceded. He looked as if he wished himself very far from here.

"It will not. And while he will ignore her anger, the King knows she is not the only one who will feel so. There are plenty of powerful men who would begin to ask themselves, if the bastard son of the King can take the throne, why should not they? There are some who claim a better title to the throne than the King himself."

"De la Pole." Parker's voice was flat.

"Aye." Bryan looked defiantly at him. "De la Pole."

"You side with him?" Parker seemed to be gathering himself as if to spring.

"I am not siding with de la Pole." Bryan's voice was a trembling whisper of fear. "Never say that, Parker. Never say that again."

Parker cocked his head. The silence stretched out. Bryan's face crumpled.

"I did go to the docks and receive a letter from de la Pole, but until I opened it, I had no idea who had sent it. I swear." He began to breathe heavily. "If I had known what that dog was getting me into . . ."

"And which dog would that be?"

Susanna felt Parker tense beside her.

Then the front door slammed open so hard, it sounded like a crack of lightning.

Bryan gave a cry of fear and ran for a door Susanna had not noticed, set in the wooden paneling on the far side of the room. He threw it open and disappeared into the dark passage beyond.

Parker stood poised, weighing whether to chase down Bryan or confront whoever had come through the front door. Like her, his need to know who continued to torment them won out. She saw the moment his focus narrowed on the closed door leading to the main hallway.

Silence stretched out, ominous and frightening. She felt tight as a spring, and Parker drew his sword and let his knife drop from his sleeve into his left palm.

"Hide behind the chair," he whispered to her, and walked toward the door. He seemed intent but unafraid, whereas she felt like climbing out of her skin.

She stepped behind the high-backed chair and sank down, peerking out from the side.

Parker reached for the handle, listened for any sound beyond, and pushed the door open.

He swore.

"What is it?" Susanna rose and peered over the top of the chair.

"No one here."

Parker moved deeper into the hallway, almost disappearing from her sight in the gloom, and Susanna cried out, "Careful! They could be hiding."

He returned to the threshold, and his eyes gleamed wickedly as the lamplight caught them. He grinned as if her concern amused and delighted him.

"There is no one here." With a hiss, his sword found its scabbard again, and his knife disappeared from his hand. "Can you swim, my lady?"

"Swim?" Susanna looked at him, dumbfounded.

"It seems the game grows deeper still."

17

The Chiefe Conditions and Qualities in a Courtier: To swimme well.

Of the Chief Conditions and Qualityes in a Waytyng Gentylwoman: To be circumspect that she offend no man in her jesting and tauntynge, to appeere therby of a readye witt.

Dusk had fallen and the gloom closed in on all sides. Parker felt the prick of adrenaline along the back of his neck as he drove the cart home as fast as the road and the weather would allow.

It had started snowing again while they were at Bryan's rooms, swiftly covering everything in a crisp layer of white. Susanna was nestled deep into his side, her face turned against his shoulder, away from the wind.

He was in the grip of some lunacy. Because in the midst of their troubles, he felt a euphoria at the easy way she leaned against him. His heart wanted to burst from his chest and escape to the glorious heights, to shout out a victory cry.

Even worse, he had no will to put his feelings aside. He

wanted to savor them, enjoy them. He must be mad, yet he could not bring himself to care.

"Do you know where Bryan will go?" Susanna's question was a warm puff of air against his cold ear.

"No." He wondered whether Bryan was even alive. If the intruder had known of the secret passage, he need only have slammed open the door and then run to the exit to wait for Bryan.

That there was no sign of Bryan's body near his building meant only that he hadn't been killed as he'd fled. It did not rule out abduction and murder elsewhere. Or torture to find out what Bryan had said to Parker.

"This has been a long day."

Susanna's words echoed his own sentiments. It was time for a tactical retreat.

The spire of St. Michael's and the entrance to Crooked Lane had never looked so good. But just in case, Parker palmed his knife. If there was to be another attack today, it would be near or at his house.

He turned into his yard.

"Ho, Parker."

Susanna cried out and Parker blocked her body with his own, his knife coming up as he faced the direction of the call.

"Easy. 'Tis Simon." Their cart driver from Dover stepped closer, raising a lantern to illuminate his face.

"Sorry." Parker leaped down from the cart and turned to help Susanna.

"You are not still dodging arrows, mistress?" Simon bowed to Susanna, and she gave him a brilliant smile back.

"Not arrows anymore. A few knives."

Simon looked uneasily at Parker, as if hoping to find it was a joke, but Parker nodded confirmation.

"But I thought after I delivered you at Bridewell, you were able to see the King?" Simon looked from one to the other.

"We were. It doesn't seem to have made much difference." Parker turned to lead the horse into the stable, but Simon shook his head.

"Don't do that. You are summoned by the King. They sent me to fetch you."

"Let us go in for a bowl of stew and a cup of wine first," Parker said. "We have been chasing conspiracies around the city all day."

Simon shrugged. "I was told you must come immediately."

"Immediately, and then we will wait for hours at the King's pleasure." Parker shook his head. "We need food if we are to go to the King tonight. I cannot fight on an empty stomach."

"You shouldn't need to fight at the palace." Simon followed them to the kitchen door.

Parker laughed. "The palace is where most of my enemies lurk, Simon. My wits need to be doubly sharp to enter that hornets' nest. To say nothing of my sword."

He held the door open for Susanna. As she stepped across the threshold, he could not resist putting a hand on her shoulder.

She turned to look at him, her eyes bright and warm. He wanted nothing more than to tuck her up safe, but instead he must drag her across the city again.

"Gather your strength, my lady. This endless day looks set to go on longer."

She lifted a hand and touched his where it rested on her shoulder. "We would not have rested well tonight anyway, with so much unresolved."

Ah, but he had planned that they would. That he would have Mistress Horenbout alone again in his study beside the fire, and he had planned to take more than just one kiss this time.

She must have read his thoughts in his eyes, because the flush on her cheeks from the cold air deepened, and she lowered her gaze, then raised it again, hot with promise.

If the King or his enemies didn't kill him, the lady before him surely would.

But for once he'd go gladly, and without a fight.

Parker left her so reluctantly, she thought he would refuse the King's call to come in alone. He stood just outside the door to the inner sanctum looking so painfully conflicted, it was as though he were leaving her in a den of wolves rather than the privy chamber.

"Call out loudly, should you need me," he told her, and then murmured in the ears of the guards at the door. With a final, hard look around the room, he stepped into the passageway beyond.

Susanna sank back down on the chair that had been brought for her when they arrived. Despite the laughter around her, the conversations of the courtiers making merry after their evening meal, every eye had lighted upon her at least once since she'd arrived.

She was too tired to care, and she looked down at her lap, not even regretting her lack of charcoal and paper. If she ignored them, she knew they would lose interest.

"I know you."

The man who addressed her, coming right up to her chair, was drunk. His face was flushed with too much wine and he looked pleased with himself, as if he carried a most satisfying secret.

Susanna felt the sudden freeze of fear. A stone had lodged in her throat, all but choking her. She could do nothing but stare up at him and hope Parker would not be long.

Because she knew only too well who he was. George Boleyn. Womanizer, rapist, pig. The last time she'd seen him, he'd tried to rape her in a dark corner of the great hall of Margaret of Austria's court.

She would never forget his face. It seemed he had not forgotten hers, either, despite the years that had passed since then.

"My lord." She did not rise from her chair but she merely inclined her head, uncaring of the rudeness.

"You're speaking English now. If I recall, you pretended otherwise last time we met."

Talking to him at all was a mistake, but antagonizing him would be even worse.

"I am here at the King's request, sir, and I took instruction in English before I came, to better serve His Majesty." Perhaps knowing she was here for the King would penetrate his drink-fogged brain and restrain him.

"And what use has the King for you, little Lowlander?" He spoke loudly, and there were a few titters of laughter from courtiers nearby, but they were subdued. She was an unknown entity, and no one wanted to risk an offense that would reach the King's ears.

She did not respond. He had never asked her reason for being at Margaret's court, in the short conversation they'd had before he'd turned on her all those years ago. She had let him strike up a conversation because she had not heard the rumors that he took whichever woman he wanted. That women should take care never to be alone with him.

Boleyn crouched down and grabbed her chin, forcing her to look at him. "I had to leave Margaret's court in disgrace because of you." Spittle sprayed onto her face, and she could not look away from his mouth, the lips red and wet, forming an ugly line.

"Not because of me." Susanna jerked her chin from his hand, but continued to look him in the eye. She was in a crowded room, and the guards were paying them a good deal of attention. She would say what she wanted for once, instead of biting her tongue. "You left in disgrace because of your behavior, not my protest at it. And I was but the straw that broke the camel's back. I heard afterward you'd already drawn six complaints before my own. You are responsible for your own disgrace, my lord."

He looked at her and she thought she saw a clearing in his eyes, a return to sobriety. Then someone laughed. Whether it was at what she'd said or not, Boleyn flinched.

"Don't you know how to speak to your betters, girl?" He rose, his hand grabbing the hair at her nape and forcing her up with him. "Come now, let us finish what I started."

Shock held Susanna silent for the first few steps toward the door, then she turned to the guards. "Help me. Call Parker."

She saw them exchange an uneasy glance, and knew suddenly they could not leave their positions. They were bound to protect the King, not her.

"Parker!" Her scream cut through the conversation of the crowd, and in the silence, every head turned their way.

"*Boleyn.*" Whoever called out did so in a voice heavy with warning, trying to rein the bastard in.

"Fuck you," he called back, and laughed. By now he had her at the door to the outer chambers, and he gripped her hair harder, bent her head back even farther as he shouldered it open.

As the door swung shut behind them, she knew she had to fight.

It was all there was left.

As Boleyn shoved her forward, she slammed her heel into his instep, glad she was wearing boots instead of court slippers. As she stamped down, she jabbed an elbow as hard as she could into his side.

He cried out but his grip tightened, his fingers digging

viciously into her scalp. He lifted her up by the hair, and through the pain bursting across her eyes and forehead, she lashed out with both feet as they left the ground.

Boleyn suddenly let go of her with a scream, and she fell to the floor.

Then in a swift, sure move, she was scooped up and held safely against a dark-clad side. Parker.

"My . . . cheek." Boleyn half-lay, half-sat on the floor, his cheek dripping blood from a thin cut from outer right eye to chin.

Parker stood with his knife loosely held in his right hand and Susanna saw a thin rivulet of blood run down the blade.

Boleyn, his eyes averted, started to get to his feet, and with a sweep of his right foot Parker knocked him down again.

"Parker." Boleyn tried for bemused irritation but his voice shook too much.

Parker's face was a cold, furious mask. He wanted to kill Boleyn. Slowly and painfully.

She wanted to kill him herself.

She took a deep breath. "Come."

Parker turned to her, and she felt the jolt of his gaze: rage and deadly intent, and something deeper, bigger than she'd imagined.

"Perhaps if you could move near the wall," he said to her, his calm voice a thing apart from his eyes. "Just rest a moment on one of the chairs."

She looked from him to the chair he indicated and back. "Parker—"

"Please." His eyes told her he would not make her watch him kill a man. But he would have some reckoning.

She moved toward the chairs, glancing at Boleyn as she did. He was staring at her, pure hatred in his eyes.

If he'd looked shaken or sorry, she would have begged Parker to leave it. But he did not, and she kept her eyes on him deliberately, and sat.

Boleyn started to get up again, and this time, Parker let him.

When he was on his feet, his hand went up again to where Parker had cut him. "You've scarred me."

Parker transferred his knife to his left hand, stepped forward, and punched Boleyn in the face so hard he fell down again.

Then he waited in silence for Boleyn to stand once more.

Boleyn lay sprawled on the floor, blood pouring from his nose. He wiped at the blood, smudging it across his upper lip. "You cross a line, Parker."

"It is not I who crossed a line." Parker stood absolutely still. He looked deadly.

"Too much to drink." Boleyn tried to shrug with nonchalance, undaunted by his position on the floor. "No harm done, eh?"

"Harm was done." Parker looked at Susanna, then back at Boleyn. "Or perhaps you enjoy being lifted off the ground by your hair and dragged through a party of snickering cowards?"

Susanna could tell Boleyn had realized what Parker planned to do at the same instant she did.

"No—"

"You said no harm done. I'll take that as reckoning, Boleyn, and by your own words, no harm will be done." Parker was beside him in a single stride, his knife out in case Boleyn thought to struggle. He lifted him by the hair, and Boleyn began to shriek.

"It seems my lady has more courage than you, Boleyn. I don't think she shrieked like a maid. She only called for help." Parker turned and began dragging Boleyn back to the privy chamber.

Susanna saw that a crowd had gathered at the door through which Boleyn had dragged her, and the people scattered as Parker headed straight at them, Boleyn squealing like a stuck pig behind him.

Susanna followed Parker, completely in thrall to his boldness. He managed to drag Boleyn halfway across the privy chamber before someone shouted, "Parker, enough."

It was the man who had tried to check Boleyn earlier.

"Enough?" Parker threw Boleyn to the floor. "I think Boleyn had a mind to rape my lady before he'd have called it enough. Any of you care to do the honors on him?"

There was shocked silence.

"Ah, my pardon." Parker's voice was pure steel. "Judging by the aid you gave a helpless woman, none of you have the equipment to do the job."

"Point well made, but enough, Parker. Finish it."

Parker looked across to her. "Is it finished?"

The room held its breath.

Susanna gave a tiny nod, her eyes on his beautiful, fierce face.

"Then it is finished." Parker walked toward her and held out his arm. "But my business with the King is not."

The Chiefe Conditions and Qualities in a Courtier: To be pleasantlie disposed in commune matters and in good companie.

Of the Chief Conditions and Qualityes in a Waytyng Gentylwoman: To make her self beloved for her de-sertes, amiablenesse, and good grace, not with anie uncomelie or dishonest behaviour, or flickeringe en-ticement with wanton lookes, but with vertue and honest condicions.

Your Majesty." Parker bowed, but he kept his hand on Su-sanna's arm. It was a battle to hold it steady. If he were to release the control he imposed on himself, his whole body would be shaking.

"Trouble?" Henry glanced into the privy chamber as the door closed, at the courtiers standing subdued for once. "The yeoman guards were right to interrupt us?"

"They are to be commended. Boleyn was drunk. He sorely insulted Mistress Horenbout, dragging her by her hair out of the chamber."

The King's expression sharpened on Susanna's face. "Are you harmed?"

Parker saw her hesitate; then she nodded. Her face was white, her eyes overbright.

"My head is pounding." She massaged her scalp. "It would have been much worse had Parker not come to my aid."

"Boleyn must heed the warnings he's been given. I'll speak with him myself. A woman should be safe in the King's own privy chamber."

Boleyn would feel the chill of royal displeasure, which would hurt him more than anything Parker had done to him. The King might have many mistresses, but he believed in discretion. And he was in thrall to the notion of courtly love.

Boleyn's actions tonight could not be considered courtly in any way.

"If it pleases Your Majesty, I would have Mistress Horenbout remain in the room with us." Parker would not stay if the King refused him, no matter the consequences.

Henry hesitated. "Our business concerns secret matters."

"I can wait outside." Susanna's voice began on a tremble but finished strong, and she drew herself up.

Parker waited for the King's pronouncement, excruciatingly aware that his future depended on His Majesty's answer. To walk out on the King would most likely get him banished from court. To leave Susanna alone outside was not possible.

He turned his gaze from Susanna and found the King staring at him.

"You take your duty of safekeeping very seriously," he said.

"I take all my duties for you very seriously, Your Majesty."

Parker spoke the truth, though even if the King released him from his duty to watch Susanna, he would not leave her.

"Very well. She can sit at my desk and illuminate some writs and title deeds I finished this afternoon while we conclude our business."

Parker opened his mouth to protest that Susanna had been violently attacked and could not be expected to work, but she gave an infinitesimal shake of her head.

"I do not have my paints with me, Your Majesty, but I can work on the designs now and paint later."

The King nodded, and gestured Parker toward a suite of chairs near the fire.

Susanna was already sitting at the King's desk with a quill in her hand, tracing a design, by the time they settled themselves.

"So, what news for me, Parker?" Henry shifted in his chair to get comfortable. "I broke off my evening entertainments and called for you because my spies bring nothing but disturbing rumors." He hunched away from Susanna and lowered his head. "I heard you are legend for the attacks you have fought off in the last two days."

"Who knows of the attacks?" Parker's voice was hard. If the King's spies had been there, why had they not given him aid?

"Again, it was told me as a rumor. What is the truth?"

"Mistress Horenbout and I have been attacked four times since we left your closet almost three days ago."

The King looked thoughtful. "The reason?"

"The reason becomes harder to grasp the more I uncover. I

can only say it seems connected to de la Pole. But even that may not be the truth." He withdrew the letter he'd retrieved from Harvey's widow and held it out.

The King took it, and there was no mistaking the horror, the rage on his face. "I *burned* this. How . . ." A vein throbbed at his temple, and Parker handed him his cup of wine.

"It is a copy, or perhaps a draft. See the lines scored through? The lack of a seal?"

The King swallowed his wine in a single gulp and brought the letter closer to his face. "You are right. Where did you come by this?"

"Harvey." This was a most delicate moment. How much to implicate Harvey's widow, how much to leave vague?

"It was on his body? Who found it?"

"His widow gave it to me." That was the truth, without going into detail.

"She read it?" The King lifted his cup and scowled at the lack of wine within, and Parker filled it from the jug at his elbow.

"She says not."

"Thank God she gave it to you, of all people."

Parker looked across at Susanna. The King still had cause to feel threatened by what she knew. Time to swing the balance in her favor. "You can thank Mistress Horenbout. Had she not insisted on going to speak to Mistress Harvey of her husband's last words, we would not have known of the letter."

The King sat back. "There are many who would have told me some untruth to reassure me or to advance themselves." He snorted. "There are some who would have kept this for leverage at a later time. You never fail me in that way, Parker. And because of it I will support you, even though you may find yourself annoying powerful men." He gripped the letter in his fist, crunching it into a ball, then threw it straight into the fire.

The message was clear. If the de la Pole conspiracy led to the highest levels of court, as it surely must do, Parker could question or harass whom he would to get to the truth. There would be no repercussions for him.

A surge of triumph gripped him. Now he had the means to go for the throat.

And he intended to use it.

———————

The bells of St. Michael's were ringing the curfew as Parker let himself into the house. The horse was brushed and stabled, and it was only ten o'clock on the longest day of his life.

"Parker?"

He whirled. Susanna stood in the doorway to his study, one hand pressed against the door frame as if it were the only thing holding her up.

He'd thought she would go to bed while he settled the horse. He'd wanted to ask her to wait for him, but one look at her pale, drawn face had quelled that impulse.

He had no more expectations of sweet kisses before the fire; the King and Boleyn had seen to that. But he would like to talk. He was too keyed up to sleep just yet.

"Is all well?" He could think of nothing else to say.

She nodded. "Thanks to you, all is well." She stepped back into the study and he followed her. She had poured them wine and laid out a platter of food Mistress Greene must have left for them in the kitchen.

He let out a contented sigh.

She smiled, the first smile he'd seen since Boleyn attacked her.

"My sighs amuse you?" he asked, quirking an eyebrow, because he wanted the glow of that smile to keep warming him.

She did not answer, but her smile deepened and she sat beside him. For a while, they sipped wine and took slivers of cold lamb and sliced apple from the platter.

It was a balm to his soul.

"Will you be out of favor? After tonight?" She spoke quietly, as if the thought had been wearing her down.

"I was never in favor. Not with those wasps." Suddenly he felt bone-tired.

"Why do you call them wasps?" Her voice seemed to come from a long way away.

"Not as nice as bees around the royal honeypot. They don't produce anything useful, and they'll sting you to death if they get the chance."

She laughed, a delightful burst of sound that roused him from his half-doze.

"There are a few who think well of me. They will approve of my actions tonight. And the King gave me even more trust after tonight—and fortunately for me, he is the only one who counts."

She leaned back in her chair, as if released of her tension, then reached out for the same piece of apple as he. Their fingers brushed, and his fatigue disappeared as quickly as morning mist under a hot summer sun.

He was fully, vitally awake.

He lifted his head to look at her, and found she was already staring at him.

"I thought . . ." His words were not as steady as he'd hoped. "After Boleyn—"

She leaned forward and placed a trembling finger on his lips. It was the boldest move she'd made in the dance between them, and he was seared by a lightning surge of heat. "Boleyn can go to hell," she said.

Parker's thoughts exactly.

He took hold of her finger and kissed the tip. Then he took it in his mouth and gently bit down.

She drew in a breath, sharp as the hiss of the sea on a sandy beach. The sound undid him.

He must have leaned over and lifted her into his lap. He only knew that she was suddenly in his arms, her thighs straddling him as he tasted her neck and her shoulder, as her hands moved clumsily to untie his shirt.

He jerked down the neck of her gown to release one hard, pink nipple, then took it in his mouth. As she arched back with a cry, he wondered, his heart stuttering at the thought, how he could ever let her go.

19

The Chiefe Conditions and Qualities in a Courtier: To fellowship him self for the most part with men of the best sort and of most estimation, and with his equalles, so he be also beloved of his inferiours.

Of the Chief Conditions and Qualityes in a Waytyng Gentylwoman: To have the vertues of the minde, as wisdome, justice, noblenesse of courage, temperance, strength of the mide, continency, sobermoode, etc.

Parker was taking her to a place she had never been. The smallest movement, even the act of drawing breath, somehow drove the fever higher.

She heard her quiet, breathy moans as if they were coming from someone else, and reveled in the sound of them. They stoked the fire, along with Parker's fingers under her dress, sliding between her legs, and his teeth on her neck.

Her head was back, too heavy for her neck to hold up, and she was panting, on the verge of some wonderful revelation.

She had thought to allow Parker a few more kisses this evening, but that was before Boleyn. Before she'd seen the look in Parker's eyes in the antechamber.

"Parker?" Was that sob from her?

His hand no longer rubbed beneath her skirts, but when she saw it was to fumble with his breeches, she could think of nothing at all except that he hurry.

He muttered a curse and she lifted higher off his lap to give him room, wanting, wanting, more than she had ever thought possible to want.

A heavy knock on the front door froze her with shock.

Parker seemed not to hear it at all and, with a groan, tugged the last of his laces free. He grabbed her hips, and despite her fright, the feel of his blunt, hard head nudging her made her shiver with reaction.

"Parker. The door." She tried to hold herself back, but somehow let him nudge in deeper.

"What?" He spoke as if in a dream.

"The door," she gasped, wanting nothing more than to inch down, now that he was right there, where she needed him.

"Door?" He stiffened as the knock came again, louder and more frantic. *"No."* He surged upward, sheathing himself deep inside her, and rested his forehead against hers, breathing deeply.

She was stretched, filled. Taken.

She felt a tremble deep within, a strange ripple, and moved, just once, against him. She bit back the scream that lodged in her throat as she convulsed in delicious shudders, and then again when Parker surged upward a second time on an explosive groan, shuddering himself.

When the eddies of pure feeling subsided, she lay limp against Parker's chest.

The knock on the front door came a third time, this time accompanied by a shout.

"They'll wake the house," she muttered. As the reality of that struck her, she jerked up. "Mistress Greene," she breathed to Parker, the thought of the housekeeper finding them like this mortifying.

She knew she looked a wanton. Her hair was disheveled, her dress up around her hips, her breasts overspilling her neckline.

But Parker moved languidly, his eyelids half-closed, his eyes drinking her in as he tucked her breasts back into her bodice, his hands lingering over the job.

She felt her skin heat under his gaze, her breasts responding to him all over again.

"Careful now," he said as he lifted her off his lap, easing her off his cock slowly. She felt as if a piece of her was suddenly missing.

"Gods," he whispered with violence as she stood weak-kneed before him, tugging at the skirts of her dress.

Susanna looked at him wide-eyed, saw he was retying his breeches. A tiny smear of blood, of her virginity, smudged his bare thigh.

"It should have been slower. . . ." He stood, his face anguished, but she shook her head. Hard.

"Regret nothing. I don't."

He looked her over, as if assessing their readiness for company, and lifted a hand to her cheek, brushing her hair off her face with gentle fingers.

Then, as the knock came again, he turned with a vicious curse and strode into the hall to answer the door.

———

An icy wind blew in with Francis Bryan, like a premonition. It chilled the heated air of the study and leached the coziness from it.

Worse, Bryan knew he had interrupted a tryst. Susanna could see it in the way he slid sly glances her way.

He even seemed amused by Parker's ill temper. He'd looked subdued when he first walked in, but his gaze had sharpened on Susanna, on her hair, and she saw the tension lift from his tight-drawn face.

She avoided his eyes and concentrated on the wine in her cup, swirling it in patterns and watching the red liquid cling to the sides.

"Your very life had best be in danger, for this interruption," Parker said, and Susanna had to fight a smile, he was so furious.

"It is." Bryan's amusement faded. "Whoever slammed the door while you were with me was waiting at the side door to my rooms."

"How did you escape them?" Parker had not offered Bryan a seat, and had not taken one himself. He crossed his arms, glowering.

"I am not without use as a sword arm." Bryan sounded so offended that Susanna coughed on her wine.

Why was everything so amusing all of a sudden?

"No. You're one of the best, but I was outside moments after you, and there was no sign of swordplay."

"My passage does not exit through the side door, but the kitchen," Bryan explained. "But I saw them lurking before I fled. They saw me too, and I assume tried to follow, but I know my neighborhood well."

"Then let us get back to what you were about to say in your rooms." Parker moved to stand behind her chair, as if he could not be away from her a moment longer. She twisted her head to look at him, but his gaze was on Bryan.

"A month or so back, I received a note at court to the effect that I would find information advantageous to me at the docks." Bryan shrugged at his own stupidity. "The note told me whom to meet and where, and a man unloading a ship from France slipped me a heavy coin. It was two pieces screwed together, and when I opened it, there was a letter inside from de la Pole."

He ran a shaking hand over his brow. "I almost perished on the spot when I realized how I'd been tricked into betrayal. My first thought was to burn it without reading it, but I wished to know what plan was afoot."

"And what plan was that?" Parker leaned forward above her, his eyes locked on Bryan.

"De la Pole spoke of a new treaty allying France and the Pope against the Emperor Charles. He had King Francis's assurance it would mean papal backing of his claim to the throne. He wanted to know if I would be with him, and he named the titles that would be mine should I stand beside him."

"Why would he take such a chance, if he did not know where your loyalties lay?" Susanna spoke for the first time, and she was aware of Bryan's sudden, sharp focus.

"That is the beauty of this trap. Who would believe de la Pole would be so careless? No matter whom I showed the letter to, they would wonder the same as you—including the King. And where would I be then?"

"Your open contempt for the English court and your behavior with Francis all those years ago has come back to haunt you." Parker spoke with no relish, but Bryan flushed crimson.

"Damn you, Parker. Have you never done something stupid in the high spirits of youth?"

Parker did not reply, which only enraged Bryan even more. He lifted his head and drew in a deep breath, trying to gain control of himself.

Something told Susanna that Bryan still did things he liked to put down to the high spirits of youth. The excuse was most likely beginning to wear thin.

"What will you do, Parker? I was told you had audience with the King this evening, and decided to throw my lot in your hands." Bryan sat down in Parker's chair, his hands shaking on the armrests.

Parker reached out and carressed the back of Susanna's neck. "I seek whoever is trying to kill me and my lady." His thumb brushed against her skin. "And I have vengeance in mind."

Bryan was a superb actor, but surely even he could not pretend such agitation. The man had gone from abject fear to anger more times than Parker could count since his arrival.

Beneath his hand, Susanna stirred in her chair, and he felt the warmth of her skin like a glow against his. Damn them all. He wished for nothing but the time to woo her.

"Your mission is personal?" Bryan broke through his thoughts with words heavy with hope. "The King has not yet sent you?"

"The King knows only the broadest details." He began to trace tiny circles on her nape. "And this evening, he gave me full authority to discover all."

"Parker, please, you must help me get out of this. I had no intention of betraying the King. Now I'm in an impossible situation. I'm ruined if I come forward, and I'm ruined if I don't." Bryan leaped from his chair and went to the window, peering through the glass and the wooden slats as if a spy lurked outside.

Parker considered Bryan's tale. If he was telling the truth, it was a magnificent trap, startling in its brilliance. His respect for his enemy grew.

How many others were caught in the same bind as Bryan? How many greedy, self-advancing idiots at court would have fallen for a similar letter to learn something to their advantage at the docks?

Plenty.

Sooner or later, someone would talk and it would come out, and they would all look guilty. And the likelihood was they would be exiled, or sent to the Tower.

And in one swoop, at the King's expense and trouble, de la Pole's supporters would have rid themselves of the King's men.

To work properly, to create the right atmosphere of distrust and tension, the King would have to learn of the secret treaty from a trusted source.

And that trusted source might well be the devisor of the plot.

"You have a safe place to stay tonight?"

Bryan had sunk into his misery, but looked up at Parker's question. He nodded. "I have a mistress no one knows about. I can stay with her."

"Good. Be off."

Bryan stumbled to his feet. "You will help me?"

"As much as I can. But only if you truly are innocent in this."

"Thank you, Parker." Bryan's bow was deep, and Parker noticed the man's step was lighter as he showed him the door.

The cold winter wind swirled around them, and then Bryan was gone.

Susanna sat where he'd left her, deep in thought.

Parker knelt at her side. "Who was on deck with you when Harvey leaped aboard?"

She started. "Almost all of us," she said after a moment.

"Doctor Pettigrew and I were watching the quay, and called out to the captain that Harvey wanted to leap aboard. It was then we noticed he was being pursued."

"Who helped Harvey aboard?"

"Pettigrew. He leaned across and grabbed Harvey's hand, then hauled him up. For someone of Pettigrew's age, it was a great feat."

"Do you remember what that archer said, the one who attacked us coming from Dover?"

Susanna shook her head. She could recall only the bolts deep in flesh, and the circling birds. All else was hazy.

"He said the man who paid him had old hands. And it has always seemed to me amazing that the archer who shot at you in the captain's cabin knew you were there."

"You think Pettigrew paid for those attacks?" She sounded stunned, as if the doctor had deeply betrayed her.

"I am convinced of it."

"Then you are saying Pettigrew knew Harvey. Was there to make sure Harvey never made it across the Channel. And it was he who was standing behind me when Harvey gave me that cryptic message for his wife."

"Aye." It was the only thing that made sense. "And once we accept that, then there has to be a close connection between Harvey's intelligence and Pettigrew." Parker rose to his feet.

"What will you do?" Susanna took the hand he offered and rose from the chair.

He began leading her toward the stairs, and their bed-chambers.

"I will have to send someone to Dover to investigate. Simon, if he can go."

She opened her mouth to answer, and he put his fingers to her lips. "But we have better things to do now."

20

The Chiefe Conditions and Qualities in a Courtier: To confesse his ignorance, whan he seeth time and place therto, in suche qualities as he knoweth him selfe to have no maner skill in.

Of the Chief Conditions and Qualityes in a Waytyng Gentylwoman: Not to be haughtie, envious, yl-tunged, lyght, contentious nor untowardlye.

She stood in the center of her room and wondered why she felt shy. Half an hour ago, this man had been inside her, thrusting. . . . She clenched her legs together at the sudden throb between them, and lowered her eyes.

When Parker followed and closed the door behind him, some instinct screamed for her to run.

She felt too much. She had given herself with relish, with joy downstairs; but the illicit way they had taken each other, on a chair in the study with Bryan pounding on the door, seemed more lust than love.

Parker was ridding himself of his doublet, pushing the buttons out one by one, his eyes on her steady and warm, and she knew he had nothing but intimacy in mind now. It made her knees weak and her heart thunder with panic.

"Come here." He shrugged the doublet off and draped it over the chair next to her bed.

She grasped her hands together, wavering. Parker cocked his head to one side, and she watched him relax, hands at his sides, palms out. She could turn him away, and he would not force her or rail against it.

She did not want to turn him away.

She stepped forward, and he took her hand in his, drawing it to his chest.

Beneath her palm, his heart pounded, and she felt the rhythm matched by her own blood. His skin was hot, the warmth radiating through his thin cambric shirt and heating her hand.

She sighed.

He stepped in closer, then put his arms around her to work the laces of her gown. The rub of fabric on her shoulders, across her breasts, as he fiddled and tugged was exquisite. With shaking hands she pulled at the drawstring that held the front of his shirt together. Then she pushed the fine fabric aside and leaned forward to touch her tongue to his skin.

"Gods." He jerked back. As he stepped away, her dress slipped off her shoulders, all the laces undone. It held for a moment on her elbows, and then fluttered to the floor.

He grinned wickedly, and the flame of the single candle on her dresser stuttered in an eddy of air, throwing shadow and light on his face. Strong, intense, and . . . happy.

She was awestruck at how Parker never affected his blank stare when he was with her. He gave himself, his feelings, into her care.

With a wriggle, she rid herself of her underskirt and then hauled her chemise over her head, standing naked in his sight.

His smile had gone. He reached out a hand and drew her closer, bent to delicately nuzzle her ear.

"I never stayed much in this house before," he whispered. "It never felt like home. Nowhere did."

"And now?" She swallowed hard, suddenly close to tears.

"Now I realize anywhere will do, as long as you are with me."

———————

Y ou was followed yesterday." Harry stamped his feet to warm them.

Parker rubbed a hand over the stubble on his chin and watched the boy trying to warm himself before the kitchen fire.

He'd thrown stones at Parker's window until Parker had heard the rattle from deep under the covers in Susanna's chamber and went down to let him in.

"Why didn't you tell me last night?" Not that he'd have been able to do any more about it than he could now, at four in the morning.

"Tried to." Harry shivered and edged closer to the flames. He took another piece of cold lamb from the plate Parker had given him, and chewed with relish. "George was following your follower. He waited hereabouts for a chance to tell you, but then you turned straight around and went out again with someone."

"He did well to hang back." Though he trusted Simon, Parker wasn't prepared to reveal his little band of eyes and ears to anyone.

"Yeah?" Harry nodded. "He waited awhile, but you were too long coming back, for such a cold evening."

"Mistress Gould do right by you last night?" Parker asked.

"Aye. Gave us a couple of rooms, pallets, and blankets." Harry rubbed his hands up the arms of his new coat. "I'm just used to waking early in this weather. Under the pier, if you don't, you might not wake up at all." He was silent for a moment, then shook himself back to the present. "I couldn't get back to sleep and thought I might as well come round and tell you the news 'fore there's more eyes on the street."

Parker gave him an approving look. He'd have liked a couple more hours in bed, but he couldn't fault Harry's logic.

Harry obviously felt warm enough at last, because he took a chair at the table, ripping into the piece of bread Parker'd put out for him.

"Give me the other news first. We can get back to what George saw." Parker sat as well and stretched his legs out. Gods, he was tired. He yawned, covering his mouth with both hands. He wondered whether Susanna had woken yet.

"Busy night?"

Harry was laughing at him, the little bastard. With a look in his eyes way too adult for his years.

Parker gave him a halfhearted glare. "What do you have for me?"

"The cove who was following Bryan on the stairs of the palace, the one Will saw at Blackfriars, works for someone who works for someone on the Privy Council."

He'd expected that, but it still felt like a punch to the gut. This could bring down a noble line. "Who?"

Harry shrugged. "Dunno. He met with a man, whispered something to him, and we decided to follow the new man— looked like he was the big cheese. He was allowed through some doors, and when we tried to follow, we were told only servants of Privy Council members could go through."

"The messenger-boy disguise is working, then?"

"They don't hardly notice us," Harry said with glee. "An' they give us food."

As Parker had been paying their new landlady for meals, he assumed Harry's delight was more in scoring an extra meal free than because he was going without. And by the look of him, he could double up on lunch for quite a time before it showed on his frame.

"Did George see who followed me?"

"No. Just saw he was behind you when you visited those courtiers' rooms near the palace, and then followed you back here. The spy seemed to think you was done for the day, and maybe it was too cold or summat, 'cause George says he disappeared."

"Disappeared?" Parker sat up straight.

"Aye. One moment he was dodging from house to house

behind your cart, and then he just vanished. George said he was watching the whole lane, that the only place the cove could have gone was your own courtyard. But then you came out not long after with that other fellow, and George was too tired and hungry to keep it up."

Dread clamped a cold hand around Parker's neck.

He and Simon had always enjoyed an easy friendship. Whether Simon had followed them or not, that camaraderie would be lost the moment Parker asked him if he had. And the loss would be felt.

Parker stood.

"Where are you going?" The meal, warmth, and early hour had finally taken their toll on Harry. He was eyeing the thick rug before the fireplace with a look he usually reserved for food.

"To ruin a friendship."

――――――――

For the first time since they'd met, they were not in accord. Susanna felt it as keenly as the wind through her clothes. She sat behind Parker on his horse and leaned into his rigid back, despite the tension between them.

The horse stumbled in the dark, knee-deep in snow. The going would be treacherous this morning—the snow lay so thick it had been impossible to take the cart, and she couldn't help but feel glad. Parker couldn't easily cut her off when she had to cling to him like a limpet.

Simon would not have betrayed them. She refused to believe it. Parker seemed to think it a foregone conclusion.

But despite their difference of opinion, there was a fragile thread between them. The beauty and comfort of last night could not be snapped so easily. As she pressed against him and tightened her arms about his waist, she felt Parker relax.

He sighed.

Her lips curved at the sound: the resigned admittance of defeat.

"Do my sighs still amuse you?" There was a glimmer of laughter in his voice.

"You know they do."

"He could have done it, you know." His words were as resigned as his sigh.

"I understand he could have done it. He may even *have* done it. But I do not think it was to betray us, Parker. I cannot believe that of Simon. Not after the longbow attack in the forest."

"I am hard-pressed to lose any friend. Simon was a particular ally."

His voice was even, but she'd long since learned that Parker could talk of the most terrible things in the same manner as the weather. He was bitterly, deeply sorry that he had to confront Simon.

There had to be a way out of this. She refused to let Parker isolate himself even more for her sake.

"Where does Simon live?"

"Over the stables at Bridewell. He has his own room, given his position." Parker turned the horse out of Crooked Lane and into Fish Street Hill, his voice low in the hush of the early morning.

"What is his position?"

"He moves the King's important goods where the King wants them to go. Sometimes that means picking up a special delivery at Dover, sometimes moving things around the city. He is not merely a cartman, more a yeoman guard disguised as a cartman."

Susanna closed her eyes and buried her nose in Parker's back, content to half-doze as he navigated through the drifts.

The streets were almost empty. The city of London stirred awake later than usual today, under the pressing dark and the dead quiet of the snow.

They skirted Blackfriars and crossed the Fleet River in eerie silence, but when they turned into Bridewell, it was as if the world of London was a reality apart.

The courtyard bustled, men shouting to each other as they loaded carts in the lantern-light, children dashing and weaving between them with pieces of furniture, pots, and food wrapped in cloth or stored in clay jars.

"I cannot believe I forgot." Parker's voice was a hush of surprise. "I . . . I would never have . . ."

Despite the horror she heard in his tone, Susanna smiled. "Never would have forgotten whatever this is, before you met me?"

She felt his chest expand under her hands and he twisted in the saddle to look over his shoulder. There was a grin on his face and a light in his eyes. "You have ruined me, my lady."

"Perhaps we have ruined each other." She smiled back, and for a moment the courtyard faded away.

A boy shouted out as he darted past them, and the horse's jerk of surprise brought them back to the muddy snow and noise of Bridewell.

"What is it you have forgotten?" Her voice was breathless.

"The King has moved to Greenwich. He wants to hunt in the parks for a few days."

"These servants are moving the royal household?" It could be nothing else. Susanna had never seen such chaos.

"The King would have gone ahead late last night. It is safer for him."

"So Simon is likely with the King?"

"Aye." Parker scanned the courtyard. "He'll stay at Green-wich." His gaze lifted to a window above the stables, and lingered.

"Do you see something?" In the weak light given off by the courtyard lanterns and the few lit windows of the palace, she could barely see Parker's face.

"Probably nothing." He turned the horse around. "We may as well get breakfast and decide who else we can send to Dover."

"Simon could still do it," she said quietly, but he shook his head.

"No. He can't."

"Why not?" She clutched him tightly as he urged the horse a little faster through the entrance gates.

"Because he's following us right now."

21

The Chiefe Conditions and Qualities in a Courtier: To delite and refresh the hearers mindes in being pleasant, feat conceited, and a meerie talker, applyed to time and place.

Of the Chief Conditions and Qualityes in a Waytyng Gentylwoman: Not to use over much familyaritie without measure and bridle.

"Where is he?" Susanna's breath tickled his frozen ear with warmth.

"A few buildings back." Parker steered the horse up to Fleet Street, then toward the bridge and home.

The sharp click of the horse's hooves on the cobbles of the bridge reminded him of all the times he'd ridden with Simon. Reminded him how much he stood to lose. Parker stopped the horse. The swish of the Fleet below and the horse's soft expulsion of breath were the only sounds.

"What is it?" Susanna leaned out from behind him to look up Ludgate Hill, sloping up before them.

They were only a few paces from the end of the bridge, and Parker turned the horse around. Then waited.

A minute ticked by. Then another. Parker flexed his hand, amazed at his reluctance to flick out his knife.

Of course he will not step out. He is not the man you thought he was.

He gave it ten more beats. As he began to turn the horse around, Simon appeared. He wore black and kept to the edge of the deepest shadows. But he came forward.

They stared at each other. It was dark enough and they were far enough apart that he could not read Simon's expression. But Parker could see the tension in him, in the way he held himself.

Simon began to walk across the bridge, and Parker lifted his leg over the horse's neck and dismounted. His knife was in his hand without him thinking of it as his boots crunched into the crystalline snow.

Susanna put a hand on his shoulder to steady herself as she slid off the saddle, using his body to help her balance. It was the easy, unconscious action of a lover or close friend. It made the moment easier.

Simon stopped just in front of them.

"Why shouldn't I cut you down right here?" Parker had meant to play it cooler, was surprised as the words seem to leap from him.

Simon tugged off his glove, then lifted his hand so Parker could see the ring gleaming on his right hand.

Parker stared at it.

"You understand why I could say nothing," Simon said, at last breaking his silence.

"Come home with us." Parker's mind was a jumbled whirl of questions. "We're going to have breakfast."

Susanna looked from him to Simon with amazement. "What was that?" She checked Simon's attempt to pull his glove back on and frowned at the ring, peering at it closely in the dark.

"It is the King's ring," Simon explained.

"That ring could save a man condemned to die for treason, even if he were being led to the chopping block when he received it." Parker spoke with respect.

Simon grinned. "Yes, but the King felt my chances were likely worse than a condemned man's if Parker should suspect me of wrongdoing." He pulled the glove back on. "This was my insurance, should I need it. I take you gladly as a friend, Parker, but I would give nothing for my chances as your enemy."

"How sensible." Parker lifted Susanna onto the horse; as she swung her leg over the saddle, he saw a quick movement in the shadows on Ludgate Hill. Pretending to tighten the saddle, he flicked a glance to the other side of the street. Yes, one on each side. Directly on their path home.

"I need to know," he said to Simon as he adjusted the stirrups for Susanna's shorter legs, "did you bring any friends with you?"

Simon's eyes widened but he didn't so much as look up at the street. "No."

"Then it seems there are some not quite as sensible as you."

S usanna frowned. There was something wrong. Parker was clearly shortening the stirrups for her, as if he meant her to ride alone, and she caught the ghost of a whisper between him and Simon. The way his face hardened, the intensity of his eyes, was like yesterday in Bryan's rooms when the door had slammed open. He was getting ready to fight. She looked down, and as if on cue, his left arm flicked and his knife dropped into his palm.

There was something very disturbing about how attuned she was to him. She had not thought of a lover and partner, a man she could share with. She had thought only of someone she could walk away from when the time came. When he could no longer accept her long days and longer nights working at her craft.

That would be impossible for her now. There would be no getting out of this without a broken heart. She pushed the desolation somewhere deep inside.

"Where are they?" she asked, and saw him jerk in surprise.

"Just up ahead, on either side of the road." He spoke quietly, as if murmuring to the horse. "Come," he said aloud. "Let us get home." He began leading the horse forward, sticking to the right flank.

"Do you think they will attack, now there are two of us?" Simon took the left side. "And is it wise to take Mistress Horenbout into the fray?"

"I would rather she be anywhere but here, but if there are two up ahead, there could be more behind us."

"True enough." Simon patted the horse and looked up at her. "Quite like old times, eh?"

Susanna shuddered. "I hope not." But it was clear Simon and Parker did not share her feelings. Anticipation swirled in them even as they kept their strides and their faces steady.

"Ride ahead when we engage," Parker told her. "Not too far; I want to see where you are. But ride out of their reach."

She nodded, hoping she could. She wasn't used to riding a horse, but this was a placid gelding, a steady cart horse. Her worry was for watching and not being able to help.

The shadows stirred on either side of the street, and two figures detached themselves like dark wraiths.

"Here we go." Simon's voice was a mix of tension and excitement as he leaped to meet the man springing from the shadows.

Parker's sword was out so fast, it seemed to Susanna it simply appeared in his hand. He gave no shout as he stepped forward to meet the attacker who sprang at him. They met with a grunt and the hiss of steel, up close to each other.

As they broke away and lifted their swords for the next blow, she suddenly realized she needed to move. She urged the horse forward, the sinister ring of steel enough to force him into a trot.

She turned him around a little way up the hill, her heart thundering in her chest, and saw Parker and Simon fighting back to back.

A candle flared in a room above the road, and a man in a white nightshirt stuck his torso out. "What in heaven's name is going on down there?"

His shout acted like a cock's crow. More lights flickered to life behind more windows, and Susanna saw the attackers step out of Parker's and Simon's reach. They turned up the hill and began to run—straight for her.

She leaned forward on the saddle. "Come on, boy." Digging her knees into his sides and flicking the reins, she forced the horse forward, but he wouldn't go faster than a walk.

"Susanna!" Parker's shout was fierce as he chased down their assailants, and hearing him so close on their heels startled them. One stumbled in his panic just abreast of her and scooped something off the ground, then threw it straight at her.

She cried out, her arm lifting a second too late as cold, wet snow came hurling at her.

She blinked it out of her eyes and wiped it off her face as Parker reached her.

"Just snow?" His eyes searched her face.

She nodded. "Just snow." She shivered.

His hand came up and his fingers curled around her neck, then he tugged her down to kiss her forehead.

"Notice how they ran when the lights started coming on?" Simon had reached them, and she saw his surprise at their intimate embrace. He carefully blanked it away as Parker's hand slid from her neck and gripped her ankle protectively. And did not let go.

"You think they were afraid we would recognize them? I could only see the eyes of my attacker; his face was covered against the cold."

"Yes," Simon said. "But there is more than one way to recognize a man."

"Who was it?" Parker's nostril's flared, eager as a wolf with a fresh scent.

"Tom Fielder." Simon smiled with dark satisfaction. "He didn't expect me here, or he would not have worn the coat he won off me at one-and-thirty last week."

"I can see why he would not wish to be recognized." Parker blew out a cloudy breath in amazement. "This game becomes truly dangerous."

Susanna couldn't help the laugh that escaped her. "You think it only *now* becomes dangerous?"

"However dangerous it was, that danger has just doubled." Simon's words were hushed, and he and Parker stood looking up the hill in the direction the attackers had run.

"Who is Tom Fielder, then?" Susanna asked. Whoever he was, he had given Simon a well-matched fight.

"He is a protégé of the Lord High Treasurer. He holds a high position at court." Simon rubbed his arms.

"I trained the bastard myself." Parker's fists were curled tight. "Keep that ring safe on you, and not far from either Mistress Horenbout or myself. It seems we will need it."

22

The Chiefe Conditions and Qualities in a Courtier: To have the feate of drawing and peincting.

Of the Chief Conditions and Qualityes in a Waytyng Gentylwoman: To be learned.

Simon hefted the saddle pack onto the horse, then crouched to adjust the straps.

"Beware of Pettigrew," Parker said, recalling Susanna's outrage when they had worked out the physician's role. Thinking of the hours she'd sat alone with him in the captain's cabin awaiting Parker's arrival, he realized the only thing that had kept her alive was Pettigrew's need to maintain his cover. He would have been the only suspect had she come to harm. "Don't be fooled by his age and countenance. He must be cold as stone to have done what he did without betraying himself."

Simon nodded, straightened up. "At least I know my enemy, which is more than you."

The way he said it made Parker's gaze sharpen on his face. "What do you mean?"

Simon cast a quick glance at the barn door, and Parker knew he was making sure Susanna was still in the house. He waited a long moment, then shook his head. "Nothing. Just take care."

"You think Susanna is a danger to me?"

"I only know you are not yourself. And it occurs to me, she had just as much opportunity in this as Pettigrew. More. Everything she has told you may be a lie."

Parker clenched his fists. "Your theory would hold, had it been Susanna who gave me most of the information, but that is not the case. And she has had not a moment to conspire with anyone since leaving that ship. I have been at her side constantly."

Simon turned to face him. "Forgive me. But before, you would have considered the possibility of her guilt. You would not have dismissed it out of hand. I say again, you are not yourself."

"How am I not myself?" Parker spoke each word slowly.

"After the fight just now. You went to her, kissed her. In the street." Simon shook his head as if he never thought to see such a thing.

Parker remembered the way his heart had pounded when he saw the two ruffians running straight for her, when he saw her face them and move the horse right at them. "When the one scooped something up and threw it . . ." He had to repress a shudder. "I thought it a rock."

"I thought it a rock myself," Simon conceded.

"If she were in league with these forces, would they be trying to kill her? Gripper told me himself she was the main target—I was just an extra bonus." Parker grimaced.

"You are thinking with your . . . heart, Parker. Not your brain."

"That is where you are wrong." Parker kept his gaze on Simon's face. "I have lived by my wits since my father died. And they have served me well. Every instinct tells me Susanna Horenbout is a treasure I should not let out of my grasp."

Simon gave a rueful smile. "In truth, I hope you are right. I like her well. But how will you keep her, Parker? You need permission from the King to marry."

Parker scowled. "Aye. And when this is done, I think he will concede I have more than earned the right to my own choice in a wife."

Simon looked away. Parker knew well what he was too polite to voice: that the King was a fickle and volatile man. He could deny on a whim, with no reason.

"You are wrong about another thing." Parker took the reins and began to lead Gawain from the stable. "I am more myself than I have ever been."

"You will need to be." Simon slipped his foot into a stirrup and swung up into the saddle. "If Tom Fielder is involved, it can only mean we are dealing with the head of the most noble family in England, bar the King."

———

You saw Norfolk, yesterday on the steps." Parker ground down azurite using a mortar and pestle for Susanna while she sat at his desk, finishing the designs on the King's writs. He had felt the strength in her wrists, the tone of her arms, as she'd rolled with him in her bed last night. Now he knew how she came by her power.

"The first man?" she asked, looking up. "The one who almost approached the coach?"

He nodded, and saw she shivered. "You did not care for his looks?"

"No. He looked cruel and self-serving."

"Norfolk is those and more." He tapped his lips. "Gripper told me that whoever was behind the attacks hated me personally. Offered a bonus for anyone who could kill me, as well as you. Norfolk should have sprung immediately to mind."

"He hates you?"

"Despises me. Loathes me. I'm one of the King's new men. I'm not a nobleman, yet I hold posts he thinks only a nobleman should hold. He would spit on me rather than talk to me. But as the Lord High Treasurer, he is forced to deal with me. As the Keeper of the Palace of Westminster, I keep the King's personal accounts. And the King trusts me." His relationship with Norfolk was cold and bitter, based on mutual contempt and acrimony. But he found no joy in the prospect of bringing Norfolk down.

"Why would he take such a risk? If the King suspects, surely he is as good as dead?"

Parker leaned back from his work, and realized there was a thin film of sweat on his brow from his efforts. "The King will behead him without mercy. But Norfolk's method in this is pure genius. Trapping courtiers with letters from de la Pole, isolating them, and then setting them up for the King to think *they* are the threat against him." He shook his head in admiration. "It's bold. Powerful. I had no idea Norfolk had it in him."

"And we stand in his way." Susanna's voice was clear and quiet.

"Aye. He cannot risk the King learning courtiers like Bryan are dupes, not traitors. His plans rest on the King suspecting everyone."

Parker picked up the pestle and began to grind again, pressing down and twisting as hard as he could. "He knows if the King sees shadows everywhere, the confusion will be incredible. And I have no doubt he's been careful to have nothing to do with those he has led out like goats to slaughter."

"But what of de la Pole?" Susanna set down her quill. "No matter whether Norfolk succeeds or not, surely de la Pole is coming with an army? Else why would Norfolk take the risk?"

Parker nodded slowly. "And we have no proof of that, no proof Norfolk is even involved, other than Tom Fielder attacking us. It is a strong reason to suspect, but by no means conclusive."

"We could let the courtiers dangle in the noose of their own making, and see if Norfolk betrays himself."

Parker looked up sharply, and saw that her face was set. She was thinking of Boleyn, he realized. Given Boleyn's relationship with the King, she was most likely right. He'd bet gold Boleyn also had a letter from de la Pole on his conscience.

It was a tempting plan.

"We don't know how widespread this is," he said, and tipped the fine-ground blue powder from the mortar into a leather holder Susanna had given him. "Much though I'd love Boleyn to lose his head over this, there may be many caught in this trap. Would you have ten, twenty suffer to get at Boleyn?"

Her face was pensive, and there was no immediate denial on her lips. "If they were in that room last night when Boleyn dragged me out, I would feel little sympathy for them."

He grinned. "I will never cross you, my lady. You are too fierce."

She smiled back. Reluctantly at first, but he saw when her heart caught up with her lips. "It is poorly done of me?"

He shook his head. "You were attacked and insulted. You have the right to ill feeling. We could let the greedy bastards fall, but will it be the best course?"

"The King is my benefactor. If he prospers, I prosper. What is best for him?"

Shock straightened his spine. She spoke like a man. Like him. And why not? She was employed by the King. Parker wanted to say she had no need to worry about her own prosperity, that he would see to it himself. But without the King, everything that was his could be taken.

She had never said what she wanted from him. She had told him she would make a bad wife. She had been honest in her reasons for trying to seduce her blacksmith. But Parker wasn't her blacksmith. And he didn't think either of them wanted a mere dalliance.

Later. All this could be decided later. He took a deep breath.

"The sooner we bring this madness to an end, the better. Waiting will only give Norfolk more time to wreak his havoc."

She nodded, stood, and shook out her shoulders. She had finished the intricate designs along the tops of the writs and had designed the complex-patterned first letters.

"Will it take you long to paint these?" he asked.

She looked at the pots of ground pigment he had made for her and smiled. "You have done well, apprentice. It will not take me long to finish."

"But it must dry before you can return it to the King?" He stepped closer and drew her into his arms.

Her lips curved with sudden understanding, and he stared, fascinated, at her mouth. "It will take several hours to dry, even in a nice warm room like this."

"Then paint quickly. I have an idea how to pass the drying time." He couldn't smile, couldn't make it lighthearted. He needed her more than he needed food or drink.

She gazed into his eyes, serious, delightful. "Should we not be doing—"

He cut off her words with a kiss. "Our enemies are all around. We take each moment as our last."

23

The Chiefe Conditions and Qualities in a Courtier: To endevour himself to love, please and obey his Prince in honestye.

Of the Chief Conditions and Qualityes in a Waytyng Gentylwoman: To have a sweetenesse in language and a good uttrance to entertein all kinde of men with communication woorth the hearing, honest, applyed to time and place and to the degree and disposition of the person which is her principall profession.

The view from the royal apartments at Greenwich over the Thames was spectacular. Parker saw the five-story keep in which he stood reflected in the water, blurred at the edges, the red brick façade bright against the gray cloud backdrop. The keep began to wobble at the top as a boat cut across the castellations.

He waited, apart, as the King looked over Susanna's work, delighted as a child with the designs and colors. He didn't know another man who threw himself into the moment as much as his sovereign. Still and watchful much of the time, he could enter into play with the abandon of a lion cub. But when necessary, when threatened or merely annoyed, he could kill without compunction or conscience.

"I am loath now to send these writs out, they are so excellent." As the King spoke, the reflection in the river dimmed, and Parker looked up to see some of the sunlight had been cut off by the thickening clouds.

They were not alone with the King today. His secretary was busy at a desk, and a few members of the privy chamber were quietly discussing their business. There would be no chance to talk to him privately until later.

"Parker."

Parker turned to see Norfolk at the door. He tamped down hard on every emotion surging through him and bent in a shallow bow. He did not answer or make any move to join Norfolk.

He had often thought that if the Grim Reaper had a face, it would be Norfolk's. His eyes were like smooth onyx in a face that showed cruelty and power in every line. His nose dominated it like the beak of a vulture.

He had a mind as twisted and brutal as the thugs on the docks, the only difference between him and them was the veneer and gilding of wealth and ancient lineage.

Norfolk had often said with contempt that the King could make noblemen, but he could not make gentlemen. The irony of his statement had never been lost on Parker.

As Norfolk was forced to make his way across the room to him, Parker realized he even moved like a thug, flicking his eyes around the room for any threat as he stalked forward, his fists clenched and ready.

"Norfolk." The King's call forced him to turn from his

course. "I need a word. And you must see the work of my Flemish painter." The King gallantly bowed to Susanna in dismissal, and as she curtsied in return and turned to Parker, Norfolk jostled her, making her stumble.

Norfolk threw a quick glance over his shoulder as he did it, giving Parker a death's-head smile. The meaning was clear. He could get at her anywhere.

Parker straightened, drawing everything in him into a tight coil. To attack, to eviscerate, to tear limb from limb—all possibilities presented themselves.

"Most poorly done, Norfolk." The King's words were sharp, his hand coming out to take Susanna's elbow. "You think my rooms too small, that you must knock my painter over to approach me?"

Norfolk took a step back, and Parker had regained enough control of himself to see the fury in the King's eyes.

Henry prized grace and elegance, courtly manners, romance. Norfolk was a boor whose only accomplishment was hunting deer and whose idea of courtly romance was to beat his wife when she complained about his mistress being given quarters in her home. He would never understand why the King had opened his court to men who were not noble, and hadn't the self-knowledge to realize that without his title, he would never have been welcome there himself.

"My pardon, mistress." The apology was forced from stiff lips and bore no sincerity.

"Your Grace." Susanna gave a curt nod and stepped away

from Norfolk as if he had the plague. She walked toward Parker, the bravado gone from her face now that only he could see, and he took her hand and kissed it.

He looked up and saw Henry watching him, an indecipherable look in his eye.

He lowered his own in deference. "When you have a moment later, Your Majesty, I would have a word."

The King nodded and made a shooing gesture with his hand. "I will take care of business now, and then I refuse to leave my hunting any longer. We will speak tonight, Parker." He turned to his desk, Norfolk by his side; but as Parker began to escort Susanna from the room, the King looked over his shoulder. "I have not forgotten what I promised you the other night, Parker. Do what you must."

Parker bowed in response, and his eyes went to Norfolk, who stood frozen.

He smiled at his enemy as he answered the King. "I will do whatever needs doing."

The gardens of Greenwich were magnificent.

"Like the palace gardens of the Burgundian Princes," Susanna marveled. "The red brick of the façade is also similar to the palaces of my home country."

Parker looked at the gardens as if seeing them for the first time. "They are fine enough."

Susanna smiled. "You would prefer them more rambling

and wild? With many colors and scents, rather than laid out in elegant rows?"

He stopped short, and stared at her. "Aye. I would prefer that."

A shout came from ahead of them, the kind of whoop given in victory, and Parker took her elbow as they went forward. They turned the corner of the high hedge they were following, and came upon four men bent over a game of dice.

"These four look desperate enough to have a de la Pole letter each in their pockets," Parker murmured. "And they do say misery loves company."

The men were seated in a small open-sided pavilion, and looked incongruous in their setting. Their faces were rough from lack of a shave, and their eyes were red. Susanna guessed they had not slept the night before, nor visited their chambers to change. Their dark evening clothes were out of place in the light, snow-dusted garden setting.

Their merriment stopped as soon as they caught sight of Parker, and Susanna could see from the lack of lingering amusement in their eyes and on their lips that none of the whoops of delight she had heard had been genuine. These men were determined to seem jolly, no matter what their true circumstances.

"Gentlemen." Parker gave a shallow bow, and Susanna followed his lead, sketching a curtsy.

"You have been scarce this last week, Parker." The man who spoke, a young nobleman with a handsome face and dark hair and eyes, rested his chin in his palm. Susanna thought a moment or two of silence would send him to sleep. He looked hollow-eyed and his words were slurred.

"I have been kept busy by my loyalties to the King." Parker spoke the words without inflection, but the men's attention seemed riveted on his face.

"What business is afoot?" another asked with frightening intensity, as if Parker held the key to his doom.

They all seemed wound tight as springs, but not united. Each was alone in his misery.

"I do not discuss the King's business openly." The feeble sun wedged a finger of light through the low gray clouds, and Parker shaded his eyes. "But perhaps if you would speak with me privately, Neville? If each of you would speak with me privately?"

Susanna realized with a sharp pang of joy how much she'd missed the sun. Spring wasn't far off, but this winter had dragged on for so long. It had begun early, and looked set to stay late. This weak beam reminded her that the cold would end, though. Eyes closed, she tilted her head to feel the gentle fingers of warmth on her cheeks and forehead, and smiled.

After a moment, she became aware the men had fallen silent. She lifted a hand to her eyes and opened them to find Parker and all four courtiers staring at her.

Had she done something wrong? She cast a quick look at Parker, suddenly aware again that she was on foreign soil and did not know all their ways.

But Parker did not look aghast; he looked stunned.

Confused, she glanced at the other men, who stared back at her, mouths open.

"You are illuminated," Parker said at last, and Susanna realized the sunlight had narrowed to a thin beam, and that she stood in a small pool of pale gold that caught the bronze velvet of her gown. Unwilling to step out of its warmth, craving every moment of it, she smiled at Parker.

"You need gold in the pattern for a work to be considered a true illumination." She lifted her hands, and felt the warmth of the sun on her palms. "But I will take this gold over the real thing at the moment. It lifts my spirits."

"My pardon, but who *are* you, mistress?" The question was asked by the man Parker had called Neville, his tone hushed. He pushed back in his chair and stood.

Susanna considered her answer. It was no secret, yet Parker had consistently refused to introduce her. She glanced across to him, and saw he was looking at her with a steady, intense look she did not know how to read.

She lifted her hand, palm up, giving him permission to answer as he saw fit, and he turned back to Neville.

"I'm so tired." The youngest one, the man who had spoken first, rose to his feet, knocking over a flagon of red wine as he stumbled to get out of his chair. "Perhaps she is an angel of mercy." His hand, resting on the table, was in a pool of red wine, and with a cry of shock he leaped back a step, falling over his chair and landing with a thump on the wooden floor of the pavilion. He began to weep, a quiet sound in the absolute stillness. "I am in grave, grave trouble, my lady angel."

Susanna heard the desolation in his voice. "You were tricked into accepting a letter from someone at the docks, and now it looks as though you are a traitor," she said.

The words were barely out of her mouth when Neville leaped from the pavilion, grabbing her in a stranglehold. She felt the press of a knife below her right ear as he held her against him, using her body as a shield against Parker. "What do you know of this?" His words were snarled, wild, his breath hot and feral on her neck.

Susanna reached deep within, found calm and courage. She stared at Parker, willing him to look at her, to see beyond the gales of fury howling behind his eyes.

"Parker." She spoke his name the way only a lover could. She hid nothing from him in that one word, and she saw him blink.

He began to stalk forward, so intense that Neville twitched behind her and his knife nicked her flesh.

Parker stopped short, his eyes on her neck, and she felt a tickle of blood running down to pool above her breastbone.

"I can help you in this matter, Neville." Parker spoke so low that everyone strained forward to hear him. "But if you do not step away, if you do not take your filthy hands off her, I will break you. I will denounce you. I will use every resource at my disposal to have you up at Traitor's Gate."

Neville tensed, and then he stepped back, breathing heavily.

The young nobleman was still on the floor in a growing puddle of red wine, but the other two men had risen slowly from their chairs and were very quiet. Weighing everything, undecided what to do.

Susanna felt light-headed all of a sudden. She lifted a hand to her neck, and met Parker's gaze.

With a curse, he closed the distance between them, lifting her up and setting her farther from Neville. She leaned into him, but he set her on her own feet and turned back, muscles bunched, and punched Neville in the face.

24

The Chiefe Conditions and Qualities in a Courtier: His
conversation with women to be always gentle,
sober, meeke, lowlie, modest, serviceable, comelie,
merie, not bitinge or sclaundering with jestes,
nippes, frumpes, or railings, the honesty of any.

*Of the Chief Conditions and Qualityes in a Waytyng
Gentylwoman:* To come to daunce, or to showe her
musicke with suffringe her self to be first prayed
somewhat and drawen to it.

Neville looked up at him, nose bleeding, his gaze surprisingly clear and focused. "Your pardon, Parker. I am at
my wits' end. I should never—"

"No, you should not." Parker extended a hand. "It will
never happen again." He tamped down the desire to hit Neville again as he hauled him up, and Neville must have seen the
flicker in his eyes, because he stepped away hastily, fumbling
for an overstitched kerchief for his nose.

"Your pardon, mistress. I . . . your pardon."

Parker curled an arm around Susanna and brought her
close to his side. She had been so calm, so sure of him. He
could not help shuddering in a breath and stroking back her

hair with his hand. He saw she had taken out a small square of white linen and was dabbing at her neck. It had almost stopped bleeding.

"I understand you are in trouble, sir." Her gracious response had them all eyeing each other nervously.

"What do you know of our troubles, Parker?" Guildford asked.

It was an interesting little foursome, Parker thought. It did not seem they had confided in each other. Habit and the bonds of loyalty had drawn them together in their darkest hour.

"My lady"—he gestured with his hand—"the boor who just cut you with a knife is Edward Neville. He was with Francis Bryan in Paris many years ago, throwing stones at French peasants like cruel boys with the King of France."

"We were drunk, Parker. We were fools." Neville's gaze slid away from Susanna, and Parker was pleased to see high color on his cheeks. Let the bastard squirm.

"Sitting on the floor is William Carey, George Boleyn's brother-in-law." The real reason Norfolk had picked Carey must be that his wife, Mary, had been the King's mistress up until a short time ago.

"Then we have Henry Courtenay, Earl of Devon, the King's cousin, and Henry Guildford, Master of the Horse and one of Bryan's brothers-in-law." They were a tight little group. All well-liked by the King, all perfect for Norfolk's plan.

"Sirs." Susanna curtsied, and his heart lurched. She was a rich tapestry in the flesh. Every color, every inch of her, glowed bright. She did look like an angel before the jaded, ragged men before her.

"Mistress." Guildford was the only one with the presence to bow. "You are saying you know we are innocent in this, Parker?"

"I am not sure of innocent, but I know you are no traitor to the King."

Guildford sat down slowly, and Parker saw him lean back in his chair, the most relaxed he'd been.

"You were all chosen for reasons I think you can work out for yourselves."

"And you? Where are you in all this? Who plots against us?" Courtenay spoke for the first time.

Parker shook his head. "Not against you."

Guildford sat up straighter, suddenly alert. "Against the King? But how?"

"Think, Guildford. Soon, someone will talk, someone will find out about the de la Pole letters and tell the King. And one by one, he will send the culprits to the Tower."

Carey moaned.

"Then, when he has rid himself of all his loyal supporters, when he is close to despair at the perceived betrayal, suddenly de la Pole descends with an army. And the viper within, the one who sent you to the docks for those letters in the first place, strikes in the heart of the palace."

"'Sblood." Neville stumbled back and collapsed on his chair. "God's teeth."

Carey moaned again. "I destroyed my letter—it is the only

proof against me. I thought the whole nightmare was over, but then I received a note under my door yesterday morning. It said a letter had been found addressed to me from a certain Richard living in France. That I shouldn't be so careless with my correspondence." He groped for the chair and pulled himself off the floor. "I burned that letter in the fireplace. How did they know? How do they still have it?" He sprawled onto his seat and buried his head in his hands.

"A good question." Parker offered Susanna Courtenay's chair, and she sank down on it in relief. His fury at Neville surged again, and he forced it away. "The only proof against you is the letter. Destroying it is all any of you need do to be free of this, if you were truly traitors, and whoever designed this trap knows that well."

Neville cleared his throat. "I got a note under my door yesterday. Said the same thing as Carey's."

"But you did not destroy your letter?"

Neville shook his head.

"Guildford? Courtenay?"

"It seemed proof of some plan against the King," Courtenay said, "and I wanted to keep it to show him, but also realized every finger would be pointed at me if I did so."

"The plotter decided to show his hand. Increase the pressure. Prove to you that no matter whether you destroyed the letter or not, he has you."

"You know more than you are telling us, don't you?" Guildford watched him steadily.

Parker shrugged. He would not deny it. "I don't trust you.

But I can tell you this: when the King feels threatened he lashes out, and I may not be able to persuade him of your innocence. So do not talk of this or do anything foolish."

Neville nodded in agreement. "Not even your testimony will be enough to save us if the King feels cornered. No one will hear anything from me."

"Come, my lady, we do not have a moment to lose." Parker held out his hand and helped Susanna from her chair. As they stepped from the pavilion, he bent down and spoke softly in her ear. "It is worse than we imagined. These four are usually calm, steady men and they are near breaking. I do not like to think how close to the edge other, less stable men of the court are, who have also been duped."

"You think someone will confess in his cups? Or behave like Carey?"

Parker nodded. That's exactly what he feared. "This house of cards is about to collapse."

The music was merry, and Susanna's eyes were drawn to the players, sitting on a raised platform at one end of the room. With surprise, she recognized the flute player, a musician from Ghent she'd met at Margaret's court. She dropped into a curtsy and he gave her a nod, trilling high and sweet on his flute.

Parker was scanning the room, his face set in stone. It was the most honest expression at the revelry. All around them people laughed and danced, but Susanna sensed a note of desperation to the gaiety. It set her on edge and she smoothed down her dress, the finest in her trunk, and fiddled with the gold chain and pomander attached to the girdle at her waist. She knew she looked well.

"Parker." A woman reached out and touched Parker's arm.

She was the most exquisite creature Susanna had ever seen. She could picture the woman at a pool in some green wood, talking with the trees, rising from the water like a nymph. Susanna could paint the ash wood the same white as her blond hair, the pool the same blue as her eyes, the shimmer of sunlight on the water the same pearl as her skin.

"My lady." Parker bowed, then took Susanna's elbow and drew her closer to him. He seemed wary.

Susanna curtsied to the woman, who did the same. Neither lowered her eyes as custom dictated.

"You have been scarce this last week, Parker. But perhaps the lady on your arm is the reason?" The woman smiled beguilingly, and Susanna held back a gasp. Her beauty was an unstoppable force. She could surely tempt birds from trees and men from their common sense.

"I would like nothing better than a week to court the lady at my side, Lady Carew," Parker said, calmly.

"You would?" Lady Carew was taken aback, Susanna could see it in the way her eyes darted away for a moment, as if to regroup.

"Aye." He drawled the word. "But all manner of things conspire against giving me the time I need."

"Well." Lady Carew turned her smile upon Susanna, who found herself unable to stop staring, trying to imprint the way the mouth, the eyes, and the cheeks all moved together to create the impression of bright interest and pure loveliness. "It seems you have succeeded where many a lady of court has failed, mistress. For Parker has never openly admitted a desire to woo before. You must give me your name."

There was an uncomfortable silence.

"For now, I wish the lady who has captured my regard to remain my secret," Parker said.

"How ungentlemanly of you, sir. Those are not the rules of courtly love."

Parker smiled. "You and I both know there is no such thing as courtly love in this place. The rules are followed, but they have no meaning. It is mere game-playing."

Lady Carew's mouth pursed in a pretty pout. "You would not let the King hear that."

"I would." Parker took a step away, Susanna still anchored to his side. "That is my strength. He would laugh. The veneer of courtly love is thin in this place. You more than most know what truly lies beneath the surface."

Susanna saw the flare of temper in those pool-blue eyes, a quick downturn of the mouth before order was restored. "You are a boor, Parker." All coquetting was gone.

"Perhaps. But an honest one." He bowed a farewell, but as she turned away, he leaned forward. "Have you seen Fielder?"

A blue flame burned in the look she gave him over her

shoulder. She had not mastered her temper fast enough. "I saw him at the gaming tables."

"My thanks. Please give my regards to your husband."

It seemed he could not have said anything to make her more furious. Her frame shuddered as she suppressed her anger. Her hands clenched, her neck stiffened, her back drew straighter.

This was an even better painting: *Outward Beauty Fighting Inner Beast*.

"Who *is* that?" She watched Lady Carew laugh prettily as a courtier raised her hand to his lips. She seemed oblivious to them, though a moment ago she had clearly wished them to the devil.

"That is Francis Bryan's sister, Elizabeth Carew."

Susanna suddenly understood why she had seemed vaguely familiar.

"She is also the wife of Nicholas Carew, the best jouster in England, and one of the King's closest friends."

There had to be more to it than that. "And?"

Parker slanted her a look, his lips quirked in a smile. "And the King's mistress."

25

The Chiefe Conditions and Qualities in a Courtier:
Not to be rash, nor perswade hymselfe to knowe the
thing that he knoweth not.

*Of the Chief Conditions and Qualityes in a Waytyng
Gentylwoman:* To sett out her beawtye and disposition of person with meete garmentes that shall best
beecome her, but as feininglye as she can, makyng
semblant to bestowe no labour about it, nor yet to
minde it.

"Can you see Harry?" Susanna's murmur was discreet, despite the shrieks of laughter and shouts of conversation
around them.

Parker shook his head, his eyes never still. This was deadly
earnest now, and he worried Harry would be noticed by the
wrong people.

He had accompanied them as Parker's page, a pair of invisible eyes and ears, and Parker hoped he was invisible enough
to escape harm.

He moved Susanna through the throng, avoiding, sidestep-
ping, especially when there was a danger of conversation.

Why was he so reluctant to give Susanna's name? Norfolk

knew who she was, and he was the danger. Still, Parker felt calmer knowing the vultures of court did not know her. Let them speculate. Let them gossip. She would be known to them soon enough, as the King's painter at the very least.

At last they were at the entrance to the smaller chamber that had been turned into a gaming room.

"There is Fielder." Parker spotted the yeoman as the crowd parted for an instant, and tightened his hold on Susanna's arm. He shouldered through the crowd blocking the door, the gawkers watching fortunes made and lost.

"Which one is he?" Susanna craned her neck.

"Dark hair, tall, in green." Fielder looked well. He was younger than Parker, and he had an excellent physique, broad in the shoulders, trim in the hips. But he also had the look of a man in trouble. His eyes shifted around the room, and Parker saw the moment he realized they were bearing down on him.

He froze, his eyes wide, then backed away from the table where he had been playing. As he spun toward another door at the back of the room, he knocked into a man holding a cup, sending him stumbling and his wine flying in a rainbow arc.

"Follow me." Parker dropped his hold on Susanna's arm and ducked into the crowd, half-running after Fielder through the throng.

He skirted a woman wailing as she dabbed at a wine stain across her bodice with a dainty white lace kerchief and pushed past a man muttering curses as he brushed wine from his velvet doublet. He could not let Fielder get away.

He burst through the door Fielder had taken and found

himself in a long passageway. Fielder was to the right, just turning a corner, and Parker flicked out his knife as he charged after him. He rounded the corner himself just in time to see the door midway along the passage close. A second later, and he would have missed it and run straight past it.

Making as much noise as he could, he ran to the end of the corridor, then walked back to the door in silence. He pressed himself against the wall, and withdrew his sword.

Fielder came out with a cocky, self-pleased swagger. He closed the door without looking, then shrieked as Parker whipped his sword up, blocking his way. He pinned Fielder to the door with the blade against his throat.

"Surprise, surprise." Parker grinned.

Fielder drooped, giving up the fight like a battle flag that had lost its wind. Parker was forced to push back against him to keep him upright.

"I was afraid Simon had noticed the coat."

Parker clicked his tongue and shook his head. "Not wise to wear your enemies' clothes if you plan on attacking them, Fielder. I would have told you that in your training, if I'd thought you needed something like that spelled out. Obviously you aren't as bright as I thought."

"I didn't know about Simon." Fielder's words were spoken through gritted teeth.

"You thought you'd have a two-to-one advantage, eh?"

Fielder's eyes glittered in the low, flickering light of the passageway. "For you, I'd have preferred there to be four of us."

"Ah, you flatter me." Parker leaned in with his blade, and

watched Fielder's eyes widen. "What are your instructions from Norfolk?"

Fielder's eyes shifted just for a moment over Parker's right shoulder, down the passage. He remembered that Susanna was following him and felt a moment's unease that he had left her, even for a short while, in the heat of the chase.

"Stay back," he called, not taking his eyes from Fielder.

But something was wrong. Fielder looked smug again.

Parker sensed rather than saw the arm lifting up just behind his field of vision, and it was the last thing he remembered.

The noise of the gaming room and hall were muffled in the corridor. Susanna looked left and right down the long passage, and wondered which way Parker and Fielder had run.

She heard the faint clatter of running feet to the right, and decided it was as good a direction as any. She lifted her skirts and began to jog, her thin leather slippers silent on the stone floor. These passageways must not be used by the King, for there was no runner on the floor, and few decorations and paintings hung on the walls. Low-burning candles sat in small alcoves to cut a little into the dark.

She had had Parker at her side for so long, she felt uneasy without him. Her heart fluttered like the flame of the candle just ahead.

"Mistress."

The call came from behind her and Susanna spun, narrowing her eyes in the gloom to see who was there. As the man passed in front of a lit alcove, she saw he was a stranger. And from the hard look on his face, he meant her harm.

She backed away, the flutter of her heart now a thunder, holding her skirts high so as not to trip. A wave of cold fear made her shiver as she caught the glint of a blade in his hand and realized it was too late to run. Her skirts would slow her down, and he was closer than she'd thought. He moved swiftly and with purpose.

Taking a deep breath, widening her stance, she decided to stand her ground, her mind seizing thin straws of possibility on how to defend herself. She grasped the girdle about her waist and felt the heavy pendulum swing of her copper pomander at the end of it.

Her pursuer seemed confused that she had halted, and his steps slowed. He approached more cautiously, and she used the time to unclasp the chain. She tested the weight of the pomander with a little jerk. When he was within striking distance, she gathered her courage and stepped forward with a cry, swinging the chain back and up in an arc.

He jerked with surprise at her shout, his gaze fixed on her face, and the pomander came out of the darkness at him, striking his left temple.

Susanna did not wait to see what damage she had done. Still clutching tight to the chain, she turned and ran, feeling a scream building in her chest.

Where was Parker?

At the turn in the corridor she risked a quick look back,

and saw the man kneeling on the floor, one hand against the wall to steady himself, the other raised to his head. It might have been a trick of the weak light, but she thought she saw the dull gleam of blood.

She switched her attention back to the passage in front of her, and despite the danger behind, froze.

Parker lay on the floor, his arm flung to the side, sword still in his palm, horrifically vulnerable. Above him, two men stood in quiet argument. One was Tom Fielder. With a jerk of impatience, his companion dropped to one knee beside Parker and raised his knife. Lifting it up and to the left, he grasped Parker's chin and tipped it back to give him better access.

"No!" Susanna ran at Fielder's companion, the pomander whirling in a solid copper blur at her side.

The man stopped, his mouth open, and Susanna leaped, screaming like a banshee from a dark bog. She heard the crack as the pomander connected with the bastard's skull, the blow so hard that the copper casing split open and the perfumed oil within filled the air with the scent of ambergis and cinnamon.

Her hand shook as she drew back her chain to make another strike, but as her arm swung up, it was grabbed viciously from behind and twisted up behind her back. She let out a cry of pain.

"What a mess." It was the rough voice of the man who'd been pursuing her. He hitched her arm an inch higher, and Susanna had to pant to keep from blacking out.

Fielder stood with his mouth open. "Norris. What happened to your head?"

"This little bitch did. Same way she took down Smithy."

Through the lights dancing before her eyes, Susanna saw that Smithy lay unmoving beside Parker.

Her terror made it difficult to think. She drew in a deep breath and tried to calm down. She had to get help for Parker. She had to escape.

"What do we do?" Fielder hunched his shoulders, shooting a nervous look at Susanna.

A shout of laughter floated down the corridor, and the noise of the revelry rose as a door from the hall was opened. Someone was coming.

"Help!" Susanna screamed as loud as she could, hope blossoming.

Norris's hand clamped over her mouth, and she bit his palm as hard as she could.

"Argh!" He shoved her forward and she fell onto Smithy and Parker, pain dancing down her arm as if it were on fire.

She rolled onto Parker's chest, pressing her ear to his breast, and heard the steady drum of his heart. Her left hand brushed something hard on the floor beside him and she caught hold of it with her fingertips as she was hauled up again.

Parker's knife.

She cried out as Norris wrenched her injured arm again, using the noise as a distraction as she pushed the knife up her sleeve as far as she could with one hand, forcing it under her tight undersleeve. She shivered as the blade rubbed against the thin skin of her inner arm.

To have a small chance of saving herself, she would have to make a blood offering.

The laughter from the adjoining corridor had turned to shouts and teasing, and one of the revelers broke into song.

"Leave Parker and Smithy. We can kill her somewhere quiet." Norris shoved her past Smithy, who had begun to moan and flutter his eyes as he came around. Parker's form was still.

"Leave Smithy?" Fielder clearly didn't like that. Didn't like the implication that they were all disposable. His look hardened.

"Carry him then, if you like." Norris pushed her forward, and with nothing to lose, Susanna began screaming again.

"Help! Help!"

Norris's blow landed just above her ear, making her ears ring.

Pain washed over her in waves, her knees buckled, and she crumpled to the floor. The world retreated, sound coming to her as some distant thing.

Norris spat in disgust and lifted her up, his fingers digging into her waist and back. He started down the passageway, half-carrying, half-supporting her.

"Help me!" His shout sounded as if it came from two fields away.

Fielder had obviously left Smithy to take his chances because he was empty-handed, and he took hold of her legs around the knees. The world tilted as Norris and Fielder carried her as if she were a rolled-up Turkish rug.

As they turned the corner at a jog, Susanna managed to twist her head for a final look at Parker, and saw four young courtiers standing beside him, looking at her with their mouths open.

26

The Chiefe Conditions and Qualities in a Courtier:
Not to seeke to come up by any naughtie or subtill
practise.

*Of the Chief Conditions and Qualityes in a Waytyng
Gentylwoman:* To have a good grace in all her do-
inges.

"Parker."

Someone was slapping his face. Each successive call of
his name seemed more urgent, each slap a little harder.

Parker batted the hand away and opened his eyes, squinting in the dim light.

"Denny?"

"Aye. At least your brain is not addled."

"What—" Shock punched an icy fist through his chest and
grabbed hold of his heart. "Susanna?"

"Your lady?" Denny leaned back on his heels. "I fear I have
bad news."

Parker struggled to his elbow and tried to drag himself to
his feet. With a start he saw a man beside him, struggling

against two finely dressed young courtiers sitting on his chest.

"What happened?"

"We were on our way along this passage to visit a . . . young lady and her friends for an . . . intimate visit. We were laughing and singing, and your lady might have called out a dozen times before we heard her. But that last scream . . ." Denny rubbed a shaking hand across his forehead. "It was a scream of desperation. It cut through our wine haze."

Parker felt dread sinking in him like the weights of a drawbridge, cutting off all possibility of hope.

"We ran, fast as we could. One fellow was trying to help up his friend here, the other was hauling your lady down the corridor. When the rogue saw us he abandoned his friend and they both disappeared around the corner, carrying the lady between them."

"Did you see who they were?"

"One was Fielder." The fourth courtier, standing beside Denny, sounded subdued. "I thought he was a weasel, but now I have the proof of my own eyes." He hiccuped, and peered at the floor with bleary eyes. Then he bent and picked up a gold waist chain with a cracked pomander attached.

"Is this your lady's?"

Parker reached out to take it. It was Susanna's. There was blood on it, and his fingers came away sticky with perfume. He felt the gaping chill of fear and a wave of dizziness.

"You did well to injure this cove before you were overcome, Parker." Denny's voice was full of admiration.

Parker looked at the man, blinked his eyes to clear his sight, and finally recognized him as the man Will had pointed out on the stairs of the palace, following Bryan.

"I didn't." He looked at the pomander dangling from his hand, and back to the bloody mess on the side of the man's head.

Susanna.

"Take this bastard to the Knight Marshal, and have him kept until I can question him. Which way did they go?"

"Down the corridor and to the left."

Parker gave a quick bow, and staggered as his world spun again. He waited a moment until the floor stopped moving, and then searched the ground for his weapons.

He picked up his sword, but could find no trace of his knife. It could be anywhere in the shadows and he didn't have the time to look for it.

Without a word, he knelt next to Fielder's accomplice, and the man flinched. But Parker only reached across to grab the knife beside him.

This time when he stood, the world rocked a little less violently.

"Surely you cannot go as you are?" Denny called after him as he staggered down the passageway, hand against the wall for balance. "Wait until you can stand straight, man. One of us can go with you."

Parker waved him away. They were drunk, and he couldn't risk any of them discovering the extent of this plot. "No time to lose," he called back.

For Susanna Horenbout, he'd run into the very jaws of Hell.

––––––––––

They meant to kill her, quickly and privately, and her only chance was to make it slow and public.

She relaxed her body, turned herself into a dead weight, and a thrill of satisfaction overcame her fear when Fielder stumbled.

Norris tripped in reaction, and his hand slipped from over her mouth.

She screamed.

Norris deliberately dropped her headfirst onto the stone floor, but she lifted her head in time and her shoulders and back took the impact, sending shocks of pain through her body.

She lay stunned a moment, her legs still loosely held by Fielder, but Norris was already bending to haul her up again. Using her right leg against Fielder's hip as a brace, she kicked her left hard up between his legs, arching her back to get power behind the blow.

Fielder made a tiny squeal of sound, his face white, and he dropped her, curling over his groin in a strange, slow movement.

"Pull yourself together." Norris spoke through gritted teeth, each word ground out in frustration.

Susanna let him lift her partway up, and when she judged the angle right, she twisted in his hands, scrabbling to get her legs under her. She ducked beneath his arms and staggered a few steps forward before she broke into a run.

"Lucifer's bones!" Norris's shout echoed through the passageway, his rage in every syllable. He would be vicious if he caught her.

The thought gave her an extra spurt of speed.

Norris was not far behind her, fueled by pure hatred.

Ahead Susanna could hear murmurs and the discordant clang of copper, and pushed herself even harder.

"No, no, no." Norris was so close she could hear him panting the words, almost moaning them, as she reached the large door.

It was closed, and she wasted precious seconds pushing down the catch, pulling the heavy oak toward her.

Norris was on her. As his arm came up to strike, she threw herself forward, and though his fist connected with the back of her head, she was through. With a wild cry, arms flailing, she pitched headfirst into the room, her forehead hitting the floor with a sickening crack.

She lay panting like a wounded animal, and all about her she saw the black-slippered feet of small children dressed in long red and white robes. Then the much larger slippers and robes of a clergyman blocked her view.

"What is this?" The voice that spoke was strong and authoritative.

Susanna felt her grip on the world slipping away. Her hand lay beside her face, just next to her cheek, and it seemed to waver, even though it was pressed flat against the floor.

She closed her eyes to stop the dizziness, and was sucked into oblivion.

———————

P arker came upon Fielder faster than he'd anticipated. He was up ahead, his back turned, limping as if injured.

He must have heard Parker because he glanced over his shoulder, and his eyes widened with shock.

Parker was moving fast. As long as he focused on something the ground stayed where it should, and Fielder made an excellent focal point.

Fielder stumbled to a halt and turned, his hand tightening on his sword hilt.

So he wanted to fight it out? Without hesitation, Parker drew back his arm and threw the knife he'd taken off Fielder's friend. It flew straight, and buried itself between Fielder's heart and his shoulder, bringing him down like a stag taking a bolt.

Fielder made a keening sound and scrabbled across the floor to lean against the wall, legs spread-eagled in front of him. He looked at Parker with hopeless eyes.

"Where is she?" Parker knelt beside him and closed his hand around the knife handle. He eased the knife out a fraction.

"No," Fielder choked, gasping and blinking away tears. "Don't. I'll bleed to death if you take it out."

"I don't care whether you live or die, Fielder, so tell me where she is."

"Escaped." Fielder's hand fluttered around the knife, wanting to hit Parker's hand away.

"And the bastard who was with you?"

"Norris went after her."

Parker tightened his grip on the knife, ready to pull.

"No. Take mine." Gasping like a fish, Fielder scrabbled at his belt, then held up a good knife.

"If I see you again, I'll kill you." Hearing the faint cry of a woman farther along the rabbits' warren of passages, Parker broke into a run.

The Chiefe Conditions and Qualities in a Courtier:
Not to covett to presse into the Chambre or other
secrete part where his Prince is withdrawen at any
time.

*Of the Chief Conditions and Qualityes in a Waytyng
Gentylwoman:* To be wittie and foreseing, not heady
and of a renning witt.

"Parker!" John Rightwise was so pleased to see him, Parker
took a step back to avoid an embrace.

"There has been a strange incident." Rightwise wrung his
hands. "A woman fell into the room, and a man snatched her
up and ran off. I cannot go after them; the King expects my
choir to sing for him in ten minutes."

"Snatched her up? You let him—" Parker closed his eyes to
get control. When he opened them, his gaze fixed on Rightwise's
throat, and the deviser of court revels backed away, nervously.

"She leaped into the room, wild-eyed. Hit her head on the
floor—"

"Not before that cove hit her on the head first," a choirboy
said in a clear, carrying pitch.

"What?" Rightwise turned. "Why didn't you say something?"

The boy shrugged. "My da hits my ma like that all the time."

"Was she badly injured?" Parker demanded of the boy, and he edged away, glancing left and right for support.

"She was senseless when he took her." Rightwise straightened his robes.

Parker watched him readying himself for his performance incredulously. "For your sake, I hope she's still alive, or I'll interrupt your entertainment by coming in to strike you down." He turned to the boys. "Which way did they go?"

"Left out the door," a boy called out.

Parker touched his forehead in thanks, and grabbed one of the candles from a choirboy's hand as he strode back into the passageway. He was sick with fear; it threatened to overwhelm him.

A new wave of dizziness hit him and he was forced to lean back against the wall and lower his head toward his knees.

The world was a jumble of colored lights and shifting perspective, and he made a sound in his throat, almost animal, as he tried to overcome the confusion. The place above his ear where he had been struck throbbed as if it were the size of his fist.

A searing pain scored his hand, and Parker's focus snapped back in place. He looked down and saw that wax from the candle was dripping onto his knuckles.

He needed strength and clarity. Susanna was dead if he couldn't find them within himself. If she wasn't dead already.

He straightened and broke into a shambling run, his hand trailing the wall again for support. To his left, a servants' staircase wound up to the floors above and he hesitated a moment at the foot of them, but the sound of voices around the next corner drew him forward.

He turned and stopped short. The far end of the passageway was a thoroughfare between the hall and the kitchens. Servants ran one way with empty trays, while others walked the opposite way with trays loaded high with food. A man sat watching him from a bench halfway down the corridor.

Parker went to him. "Did a man carrying a woman pass here?"

The man nodded. "He didn't pass. He turned the corner, saw the crowds, and went back the way he'd come." He frowned. "But he should have passed you, then."

Parker frowned. Where could Norris have gone? Then it came to him.

The stairs.

———

Norris was tiring. He began gasping for breath and stopped more frequently on the stairs. Susanna wondered how high he intended to go.

Her left arm was so painful, she had to bite her bottom lip to stop herself from screaming with every lurching step Norris took. It was caught between her body and his shoulder in an agony of pins and needles.

She should be grateful. The pain of it had brought her back to herself, along with the blade of Parker's knife as it scraped more skin off her inner arm with every jolt. But gratitude was the last of her feelings.

Instead, she felt a primal urge to lift her body, betray her wakefulness to Norris, just to get the blade out. This must be how prisoners felt in a torture chamber. Vulnerable and helpless against the pain.

Whenever Norris stumbled or lurched, the tip of the blade pierced her skin, and she could feel the terrible tickle of blood moving down her arm, pooling in her armpit.

Norris paused on a landing, swaying and gasping. "I'm finished."

It was all the warning she had. Before she could prepare, Norris canted to one side and she slid off his shoulder. She struck the wooden floorboards and rolled onto her side, facing away from him. The shadows were deep and she used them to ease Parker's knife from her sleeve. The relief was excruciating.

Norris was muttering, so low she could not make out his words. She heard the rustle of his clothes as if he were searching for something.

The squeak of a board from the stairs below made him still immediately. Susanna's heart lurched, then set off at a gallop. This might be her only chance.

"Help!" As she called out, she rolled away from Norris until her hip struck the stairs on the other side of the landing.

But Norris was on her before she could even get to her knees, hauling her up by the back of her dress. She heard a rip, felt the fabric give as it took her full weight.

The sound on the stairs was no longer furtive. Someone was making no secret that they were running up, and Norris was panic-stricken, his movements wild and jerky as he half-flung her ahead of him to the head of the stairs.

"I hope this kills you," he shouted as he grabbed her under the arms.

She scrabbled for purchase, terrified. He was going to pick her up and throw her at whoever was running up to them, she realized. She got a better grip on the knife clutched in her sweat-slicked right fist, lifted her elbow, and scored down hard. The feel of the knife tip biting into flesh made her shudder.

Norris screamed, his hand dropping to cover his side, releasing her right arm. Susanna pushed against him, trying to unbalance him as she pivoted to find a little room for herself at the top of the landing, but he pushed right back.

"Oh no, you don't." He spoke through gritted teeth, then shoved her as hard as he could.

There were no handholds.

Susanna pitched down the steep, narrow stairs, her scream tearing at her throat, Parker's knife flying from her grasp.

But instead of the hard edges of the stairs, she slammed into warm, living flesh.

She heard a grunt as Parker took the hit, felt him stagger back and fall with her in his arms.

They landed, sprawled and tangled together, on the landing below.

"I wish you both to the devil." Norris had his sword out, and he ran down the stairs, menacing and focused. As he reached the last stair, he lifted the sword.

Parker pushed her off him, scrabbling for a weapon, but there was no time, no chance. . . .

Despair paralyzed her. To end this way—

Norris stopped, his sword still raised, a dark bloom of blood spreading across his doublet. And she saw the knife buried in his chest.

The sword dropped from Norris's hand and clattered to the floor. Body shuddering, eyes glazed, he fumbled like an old man, then sank down onto the steps.

Susanna wrenched her gaze from him and turned to look down the stairs. Harry stood one step below the landing, his hand still extended from his throw.

"I wished for a weapon, and there it was, flying down the stairs to me. It landed at my feet." His words were hushed.

"Oh, Harry." Susanna's breath hitched in her throat. He shouldn't have had to do this. Shouldn't have had to make such a choice.

He lifted his gaze from her to Norris, his face a cold mask worthy of Parker himself. "I hope I've sent *him* to the devil."

28

The Chiefe Conditions and Qualities in a Courtier: To cast the stone well.

Of the Chief Conditions and Qualityes in a Waytyng Gentylwoman: To love one that she may marye withall, beeinge a mayden and mindinge to love.

You can't let Harry guard me." Susanna stood irresolute, arms crossed under her breasts, and Parker felt desire flicker to life, despite the circumstances. Her hair was loose, her dress ripped and slipping from her shoulders.

Only the bruise on her right temple and the shadows in her eyes indicated this was not a woman recently well-tumbled. She looked for a chair, and Parker winced as she limped to it.

"I need to question the man you attacked with your pomander. I don't want to take you with me." He held up his palms in appeal. "You will be behind a locked door. If anyone should try to get in, they will have to hack their way through solid oak."

"He is too young for the responsibility. He seriously injured a man tonight. For me." She dropped her gaze to her hands in her lap. "I have been forced to commit violence since this began, but for Harry to have had to . . ." He saw the tears on her cheeks and the tremble of her shoulders.

He had avoided touching her since Harry had come to their rescue. Afraid, desperately afraid, that once he had her in his arms, he might give in to the temptation to walk away from all this with her. To leave the lot of them to sort it out amongst themselves; to kill, torture, and maim each other until the most vicious man won.

He walked to her, still hesitant, and dropped to his knees beside her. She turned to him blindly and he was lost. He pulled her from the chair and held her to him, and let her cry tears for them both.

"Harry didn't stop Norris just for you." Parker smoothed her hair back, and tangled his fingers in its softness.

She stopped crying on a hiccup. "I know he did it for you as well—"

"No." Parker set her back a little so she could see his face. "He did it for himself."

She used the back of her hand to wipe the tears away. "Himself?"

"Harry has been at the mercy of more than one Norris in his life. That look on his face when he threw the knife . . ." Parker's lips twisted. "I know that look."

She leaned into him and sighed. "I don't want to do any more damage to him."

"My trusting him to watch you will not damage him. I swear it." He pressed his lips to her temple and closed his eyes, breathing in the perfume of her hair.

A loud knock at the door snapped him from the only moment of peace he'd had since they'd arrived at Greenwich. He rose, taking Susanna with him, and pushed her behind him as he moved to the door. He didn't know when he'd drawn his sword, but it was already in his hand. He almost stumbled as he walked, light-headed with tension. Exhaustion made him feel completely detached.

"Aye?"

"It's Denny."

Parker opened the door and let Denny in.

"Bad news, Parker." Denny wasted no time. "That rogue we took to the Knight Marshal, he's been murdered."

Parker swore and slid his sword back into its scabbard. "By whom?"

Denny shrugged. "A man dressed as a Yeoman of the Guard."

"What?" Parker looked at him in disbelief.

Denny hunched his shoulders. "Seems a message came there was a drunken brawl in the great hall, but when the provost marshals got there, they discovered they'd been tricked."

"And they returned to find the body?" Parker blew out a breath in disgust.

"They left our man in a locked room, but one of the off-duty marshals said he saw someone in a green and white tunic coming out of the room."

Parker massaged his temples. Was it an impostor, or could one of the guards themselves be involved? If so, when Norfolk realized his plot with the de la Pole letters was uncovered, the King could be in danger of assassination.

"Have you found Fielder?"

"No." Denny clenched his fists. "He'd cleared out his room and was gone by the time you got word to us to find him. If it's any consolation, he left a trail of blood behind him."

With Norris insensible, on the edge of death, they had no collaborators who could link Norfolk to the plot.

They had nothing.

Parker lowered his hands from his forehead and realized they were shaking. Fatigue and shock had finally caught up with him.

"You look like you need sleep, Parker." Denny made an elegant bow to Susanna. "I am pleased to see you well, mistress. I was worried for you."

She smiled at him, a strained, tight smile that told Parker she was as exhausted as he was. "Thank you, my lord. And for your aid to Parker when he was wounded."

Denny held out something to her, and Parker saw it was her gold chain and pomander. She reached out and took it, cradling it in her palm. Denny bowed again, and Parker walked him out.

"Things are getting worse, aren't they?" Susanna said when he closed the door. "We are going around in circles."

He shrugged. "We are whittling down Norfolk's henchmen, at the very least."

"He seems to have an endless supply." She sounded beyond tired.

Parker shook himself to keep focused and awake. "I will still need Harry to guard you."

"Why? Your suspect is dead."

"That's what bothers me. The most likely killer was a Yeoman of the Guard. I need to see the King. One of his own guards is probably in Norfolk's pocket."

———

Parker pushed open the door to the great hall, and saw he had arrived just in time.

The King stood beside his chair, watching the festivities. His eyes tracked one dancer in particular. Elizabeth Carew.

There was lust and anticipation on his face, and Parker wondered for the hundredth time how Henry and Nicholas Carew broke bread together, joked and tourneyed together, with Elizabeth between them. William Carey had received an estate, payment for services rendered by his wife, now that those services were no longer required.

Parker thought of his own reaction should the King wish to bed *his* woman, and found dark thoughts of murder and violence close to the surface. Both Carey and Carew had married women not of their own choosing. Perhaps that was the key. They did not care. Or they cared more for the advancement their wives' liaisons would bring them than the betrayal of marriage vows. If he were forced to marry against his own inclinations, perhaps he would feel the same.

But he thought not.

He pushed through the crowds before the King could act on his obvious desire for his mistress and disappear.

"Your Majesty."

The King turned to him, and Parker saw irritation and impatience in his eyes. His expression changed at the sight of Parker's face.

"What is it?" He came down the dais steps.

"Not here," Parker said.

Henry sent a lingering look across the room to where Elizabeth Carew stood, laughing with a few other ladies of the court. His mouth formed a stubborn line. "Yes, here. That corner over there."

Parker nodded. In truth, it was probably as secure a place to talk as any. "There is a deep plot afoot, Your Majesty. The tentacles reach . . . everywhere."

The King turned his head at that, and gave him his full attention. "Everywhere?"

"A man died tonight. He'd tried to kill me but was overcome, and I had Denny take him to the knight marshal to be watched."

"Indeed?" The King's nostrils flared and his eyes were wide, eager for the tale.

"Someone slipped past the Marshal's men and killed him, dressed as a Yeoman of the Guard. I'll speak with the captain, but this is moving fast, and we may not uncover a traitor until it is too late."

"Who can I trust, then?" Henry looked around the room again, assessing each face for signs of betrayal.

"I am almost certain you can trust Bryan, Neville, Carey, Courtenay, and Guildford. And Denny."

"Almost?"

Parker lifted his hands. "As I said, the game is deep. Keep them around you. Call them to you and make sure they have their swords." He hesitated, looking across at the two Yeomen of the Guard at the door. "Just in case."

"Who is behind this, Parker?"

Henry did not like being kept in the dark. Parker knew that, could see it in the tight lines of anger around his eyes, in the purse of his lips.

"I don't have a name." He would not be drawn into giving Norfolk up, only to discover the bastard had buried himself so deep behind his thugs, there was no way to out him until it was too late.

"Well, find me one."

Parker thought of all he'd been through that evening. All Susanna had been through. He did not look away from the guards. "I will."

29

The Chiefe Conditions and Qualities in a Courtier: To daunce well without over nimble footinges or to busie trickes.

Of the Chief Conditions and Qualityes in a Waytyng Gentylwoman: Not to make wise to abhorr companie and talke, though somewhat of the wantonnest, to arrise and forsake them for it.

Susanna sipped her ale and watched Parker across the breakfast table. Last night they had slept together and done nothing but sleep. Curled into Parker's back, warm, safe, and floating on the edges of wakefulness, she'd recognized that the connection she had with him was better than any number of snatched couplings she might have had with her Ghent blacksmith.

Her heart belonged to him. And it would change nothing. She was not a suitable bride for one of the King's trusted inner circle.

Despite that, she had never prevaricated with him. If she had not spoken words of love, she had shown him in every other way possible. He could not be unaware of her feelings.

"How'd you manage it?" Harry asked from his side of the table, and took another huge bite of bread and honey. "The other courtiers don't get meals brought to their rooms, do they?"

"The King has made sure my way is . . . smoothed." Parker looked up; while he seemed more rested, his eyes were as strained as they had been yesterday.

They had a hard path ahead of them yet.

"I am leaving you both here." He steepled his fingers. "After yesterday, I suspect Norfolk will be feeling cornered. He won't know how much I learned from his men, and his main servant in this plan, Fielder, is gone. If I continue to press, if I make things even more difficult for him, he may make a mistake."

His face had been cold and unyielding since they'd risen late to the sound of Harry knocking.

As he'd dressed, Susanna had seen him fit his knife up his sleeve and slip a second one into his boot.

"Who will have your back?" she asked now.

Parker brought his cup of mead to his lips. "I am able to watch my own back."

Susanna raised her eyebrows, thinking of yesterday, of the sight of him lying on the passage floor with Smithy exposing his neck for the cut.

He flicked a glance at her, and frowned. "I cannot trust anyone to watch my back. All those I think trustworthy, I've sent to the King."

"You could take Harry. If nothing else, to run for help should anyone try to attack."

Harry shot her a dark look, which she ignored. She didn't want to think about what he'd done yesterday, and she certainly didn't want him to have to do something like that again. But she equally didn't want Parker out there alone. He'd called court a wasps' nest, but in truth it was more like a snake pit. They wouldn't just sting here. They would kill.

"I do not want to leave you alone."

"Then let me sit with the Queen's ladies-in-waiting. I can while away the hours teaching them to watercolor."

Parker lowered his cup, thoughtful. "You would be safe there."

"Good, then I'll get ready." Susanna scraped back her chair and looked across at him. "You and I deal well together, don't we?"

"Because I always give you your way." The mask was down, and he was smiling in a way dangerous to her knees and her heart.

"No. Because you can be swayed by common sense." Susanna grinned. "And because you give me my way."

She had never felt more foreign. Perhaps because she had not been in the company of other women, except Mistress Greene, since her arrival from Ghent.

The women eyed her with curiosity, some hostile, others merely interested. Her satchel received as many looks as she did from the maids of honor gathered in the comfortable chamber Parker had brought her to.

The Queen was ensconced in the chamber beyond, attended by her ladies-in-waiting. No sound came from behind the door, even in the silence of the outer chamber. Every conversation had stopped when Susanna was ushered in.

There was no place for her to sit. All the elegant chairs were taken, and no one seemed inclined to stir herself to find Susanna a seat.

She gave a deep curtsy. "Good day." Twenty or so faces stared back at her, fingers poised over embroidery, cups of wine half-lifted to lips. No response was forthcoming.

The lack of reaction left her off-balance, and her gaze swept the room in search of a friendly face. There were a few, but none willing to greet her, it seemed.

She turned, and was again stunned by the beauty of Elizabeth Carew.

"Parker's mysterious lady." Lady Carew stepped forward, her eyes glittering, an air of suppressed violence about her. Her fists were clenched and Susanna thought she might strike out.

A hiss from one of the ladies stopped Elizabeth in her tracks, and she collected herself, blinked, and forced herself to incline her head in greeting.

"My lady." Susanna curtsied low in response, but kept her head up and her eyes on the King's mistress.

"Now that Parker is not here to speak in riddles, can you tell me your name?" The words were spoken softly, derisively.

"I am Susanna Horenbout, come from Ghent to work as the King's painter."

Elizabeth pulled up sharply. "A *painter?*"

From her tone, she had thought something else entirely, although Susanna didn't know what. Elizabeth had no liking for Parker, so it could not be jealousy.

"My father is court painter to Margaret of Austria. I trained under him."

Elizabeth seemed dumbstruck. "And what have you to do with Parker?"

"Parker met me at the ship and escorted me to London."

"That does not explain why he is your shadow," Elizabeth snapped. "Why does he escort you about, take you to the King?"

"I am not able to tell you why he is never far from my company, my lady. I am sorry." She lifted her hands in confusion. "Why does it concern you so?"

Elizabeth's face went still and expressionless, and she stared down at her feet.

Susanna waited to be enlightened, but no explanation was forthcoming. Suddenly light flooded the room and she turned to it, grateful for the distraction, and walked to the window. The weak sunlight had broken through the clouds and was reflected off the water below.

She turned back to face the room, sat on the wide sill, and began to unpack her charcoal and paper.

She had just begun the outline of her sketch, setting each person in her place, when a shadow fell across her work.

A woman of about her age held up a velvet cushion with brocade tassels. "That sill is hard and cold." The lady wore a dress of deep blue, and her headpiece was an elaborate affair of blue velvet and lace. Her eyes kept drifting to the sketch.

"My thanks." Susanna took the offering, and saw that every eye was upon her. Most of the embroidery had been set aside, or even packed away.

"I am Lady Mary Browne. Can you show us your work?" The woman's eyes were full of delight and she clapped her hands in excitement, as if Susanna's presence lent the morning a holiday atmosphere.

Susanna smiled. "Stand over there." She pointed to a place in good light, and took out a new sheet of paper. She began her sketch, trying to capture Mary's enthusiasm in the strokes of black on white. The magic that this was possible, that happiness, sadness, or joy could be rendered in solid form, never ceased to amaze and humble her.

She worked quickly, tamping down the urge to include the fleur-de-lis pattern on the walls behind Mary, or the intricate carving of the chair nearby. She rendered the background with simple lines and concentrated on her subject, making the details of her dress, of her smile and her eyes, stand out more.

"Oh, I cannot wait any longer." Mary relaxed the pose she'd held and came over.

With a last few strokes of her charcoal, Susanna finished the sketch. "My lady." She stood and presented it.

Mary lifted a hand to her mouth. "This is . . . me."

Susanna laughed. "Of course it is you. That is who I was drawing."

A few of the other women crowded around and began

passing the sketch among them. Elizabeth Carew stalked into the group and plucked it from an outstretched hand. She stared at it for a long moment.

"You are accomplished." She sounded astounded, and curiously relieved.

"My father would not have sent me to the King if I were not." Susanna did not understand the undercurrents, but they were there. Something more was happening here. Something she did not understand.

But her sketch had dissipated any hostility focused on her.

"We thought you were the King's new mistress," Mary whispered. "You have twice been seen coming from his closet. We never thought you could be an artist. I have never heard of a woman employed as one."

Susanna knew her eyes were wide, her mouth hanging open. "His mistress?" The words came out in a squeak.

Mary smiled at her shock. "Obviously we were wrong. Some here are very loyal to the Queen, and the moment a woman goes to His Majesty's bed, she finds herself out in the cold in these rooms. Not with me, though. What are women who catch his fancy to do? Say no? If he wants them, he almost certainly gets them."

Susanna's eyes came to rest on Elizabeth Carew, watching her from the other side of the room, her bearing more relaxed now. "He does not keep each one very long?"

"No. He is discreet. He does not boast or brag, but he has an appetite. We often know when he is ready for a change before the men. He comes more frequently to visit the Queen and jokes with a particular woman more than usual. Then he invites her to take part in one of his pageants with him. Then her family starts to progress of a sudden, gaining estates and elevated duties. Most often, her father or husband or even her betrothed makes sure she pleases the King as long as possible. Squeezes every last favor out of him before he tires of her." Her voice was low.

"And he always does?" Susanna spoke equally low.

"Tire of her?" Mary nodded. "Aye. Even that one." Her eyes flicked to Elizabeth. "Beautiful though she is, she won't last much longer than the others, I'll warrant."

"Well, I am not her replacement."

Mary smiled. "We will have to go back to our favorite pastime, then."

"Which is?"

"Trying to guess who will be."

30

The Chiefe Conditions and Qualities in a Courtier: To hunt and hauke.

Of the Chief Conditions and Qualityes in a Waytyng Gentylwoman: To win and keepe her in her Ladies favour and all others.

Norfolk looked the worse for wear.

Parker stood at the entrance to the privy chamber and watched him talking with his cronies. There were dark circles around his eyes and an insincere smile on his bloodless lips.

He would be stewing over what information Parker might have managed to get from Fielder and Norris. Norfolk's fingers reflexively brushed the hilt of his sword, and Parker savored the cold thrill of satisfaction. Norfolk was expecting the axe to fall.

It eased Parker's sense of failure, even though he couldn't touch Norfolk yet. He needed more. Much more.

He angled across the room, and Norfolk started at the sight

of him. The nobleman edged away from his place within a tight knot of the old guard, and looked right and left. Parker could almost see the cogs turning in his head.

There was no possible advantage to Norfolk in a confrontation in this room, and no escape, except into the King's inner sanctum. Something he'd want even less than a public argument with Parker.

With no choice, Norfolk walked straight toward him, his fist closed around his sword hilt.

"You plan to battle with me here?" Parker stopped toe-to-toe with Norfolk, not giving him an inch.

"If I could get away with it, I'd strike you dead where you stand." Norfolk spoke low enough for Parker's ears only, his eyes thin slits of hate.

Parker said nothing. Norfolk must know he would barely get his sword free of his scabbard before Parker had his own blade at Norfolk's throat.

They stood a moment, two wolves facing off, and Parker noticed a hush in the general conversation. He raised his head and saw the avid curiosity, the blatant glee at a brewing argument, on every face in the room. The crows were circling.

Norfolk noticed too. Looking as if he'd stepped in something vile, he made to move around Parker, but Parker matched him, blocking his way again.

"Leaving?"

Norfolk's lips grew white in the corners. "I am your superior in every way, Parker. Let me by, or you will hear of it."

"The King has given me a free hand. But if you'd like to talk with him, come, let us request an audience together."

Norfolk went still. He raised his hand as if about to strike, then plucked at his sleeve instead, readjusting it. His hand shook.

"Let us talk between ourselves first. Before we bother the King." His voice was even lower, and Parker noticed the courtiers had drifted closer.

"Most certainly. Let us talk. Although not in any passage-ways—I fear they are bad for my health."

The look Norfolk shot him was venomous. "The gardens."

Parker nodded, and with an exaggerated half-bow gestured toward the door. "After you, Your Grace."

"I wouldn't present my back to you for every holding in the realm."

Parker rubbed the bump above his ear. "Unless you wish me to call an audience with the King right now, you will start walking."

Norfolk began to draw his sword, but Parker did not do the same. He slowly, deliberately folded his arms across his chest.

Norfolk looked as if he would fall to the floor in apoplexy. He quivered with rage, the tendons in his neck bulging. He slammed his sword hilt back into its scabbard and pushed past Parker, deliberately stepping on Parker's boot and grinding down with his heel. "You will pay for this insult, you dog."

Parker grabbed Norfolk's doublet, jerking him back. He put his lips to Norfolk's ear. "I think I've paid enough already."

The buzz of conversation in the Queen's dining hall was so loud Susanna didn't hear the first few words whispered in her ear. She jerked around at the tickle of breath against her skin.

"Pardon?" She stepped away from the woman standing right beside her, and wondered why she crowded so close.

"The Queen wishes your company, mistress." The woman did not meet her eyes, her gaze darting about the room. She hunched her shoulders, ill at ease despite the finery of her dress.

Did the Queen also believe she was Elizabeth Carew's replacement as her husband's mistress? If so, this would be a most uncomfortable interview. "The Queen wishes me to sketch her?"

The lady-in-waiting looked startled, as if she had no idea what Susanna was talking about, and Susanna felt her stomach plummet. The Queen obviously *did* believe her nothing more than a new bedmate for the King. She pasted on a bright smile. "I'll need to retrieve my satchel with my paper and charcoals. I left them in the antechamber of the Queen's rooms." They would be armor of a sort, and perhaps help convince the Queen of the truth.

"The Queen is in her bedchamber downstairs. You will follow me immediately." For some reason, the woman's words were more panicked than authoritative.

"As soon as I have my satchel. An artist is no use without her tools." Susanna was determined to have her paper and pencil with her. She cursed Mary's suggestion that she leave them behind when they had been called to a repast in the dining hall set aside for the Queen and her ladies.

As Susanna turned, she saw the woman's eyes flash, and was shocked at the pure hatred there. It made Susanna more determined than ever to get her satchel.

Mary had said some of the ladies were hostile to the King's latest mistress out of loyalty to the Queen, and this focused rage was an uncomfortable taste.

She stepped out of the dining chamber and turned in the direction of the Queen's receiving rooms, down the passage and around a corner, but the woman was once again far closer to her than she'd realized. She'd closed the dining chamber door behind them, and as the sounds of the chatter within were muted, she gripped Susanna's shoulder.

Her hold was cruel and biting, and with a cry, Susanna jerked away. "My lady, I am a painter from Ghent, here at the King's request, and I have no wish to be abused!"

Again, the woman looked startled, and she stepped back a fraction. "A painter?"

"Aye. You see now why I must get my bag. I am not the King's new mistress. My satchel is the proof of that."

The woman blinked; then her gaze focused just behind Susanna.

Susanna felt the hairs on her neck stir, and as she turned her head a hand came around to clamp over her mouth. She was pulled against a man's body, his arm as biting as a steel band.

"Margaret here doesn't know about painters or mistresses, and I know for a fact she's never met the Queen." The low voice in her ear sounded amused, the hard, cruel undertone freezing her in place. "You won't need that satchel of yours where we're taking you."

Susanna's heart thumped in panic. She tried to scream, tried to twist away, but he tightened his grip and pressed his hand more viciously into her mouth. She could smell sweat and the sweet, green scent of hay on him.

Without even a grunt of effort, he lifted her off her feet, leaving her to kick uselessly at the air.

"The way clear?" Margaret asked, her cold eyes never leaving Susanna's face.

"Aye. I paid the servants to look the other way for ten minutes." He seemed relaxed, holding her easily.

More than anything else, his self-confidence thrust a cold, roiling ball of fear into her stomach.

"Come on, then." The woman stepped ahead of them, moving away from the Queen's rooms, and slipped down the service staircase at the end of the passageway.

"Time to get you tucked away, nice and safe," the man said.

Susanna tried to bite his hand, to fling herself from him, but he was immensely strong. He held her firmly, laughing softly at her attempts as he followed his accomplice down the stairs.

Tucked away nice and safe? As she panted with exertion and frustration, Susanna wondered at his words. It sounded as if he did not mean to kill her.

Which left only one alternative.

Parker should have hidden his regard for her. They were about to use her against him.

31

The Chiefe Conditions and Qualities in a Courtier:
Not to be overseene in speaking wordes otherwhile
that may offende where he ment it not.

*Of the Chief Conditions and Qualityes in a Waytyng
Gentylwoman:* Not to mingle with grave and sad
matters, meerie jestes and laughinge matters: nor
with mirth, matters of gravitie.

I s that the call to hunt?" Norfolk swung his head in the direction of the bugle call, then turned back to Parker. The clear, full notes of the call settled over them like the snow blanketing the squat rosebushes among which they stood.

"So it seems." Parker kept his eyes on Norfolk.

"Your threat to take me to the King was a bluff." Norfolk's voice rose. "He wasn't in his closet at all, he was at the stables."

Norfolk drew himself up, vibrating anger, and Parker's sword hand twitched. "Knowing what I do about you, I wouldn't let you within ten feet of the King."

"Damn you, Parker. You go too far."

"I could go further. The King has given me his full support.

I don't need to remind you what happened to Buckingham when he was tried for treason. I heard your father cried as he sentenced him, sir. You know you are not above the same fate at the chopping block."

Norfolk blanched, his posture collapsing as he took a stumbling step back. He looked stricken. "You remind me of the worst day of my life. Of my father's life."

"One you may well relive as the guilty party this time, instead of the judge. Unlike Buckingham's case, we don't just have the disaffected testimony of staff and the foolish movement of troops as evidence. We have a full-blown plot."

"And what plot is that?" Norfolk's face was impossible to read.

"Sir." Harry's voice rang out in warning from a large lemon tree in the corner of the garden.

Parker's hand went to his sword, but the man approaching was in servants' dress, unarmed. He had a hard-edged, cocky look about him and he was well-built and strong, but no threat against a sword and knife. It was a relief.

Having pressed every able-bodied man he trusted into service protecting the King today, Parker was vulnerable if Norfolk had more accomplices of Fielder's caliber available to him.

The servant picked his way through the garden toward them and Norfolk went to intercept him, white-lipped and agitated. They put their heads together, and Parker noticed that the man stumbled over his message, a curious, pent-up energy in him.

Norfolk smiled, and when at last he stepped back, his

expression was smug. The servant turned to gaze at Parker, a long, considering look that made Parker think of cats crouched over fishponds. Parker's knife dropped into his palm.

Norfolk's gaze fixed on Parker's hand. "Put it away." He shot a quick, furious look at the servant, and the man turned and walked off at an easy pace.

"I do not take orders from you, Norfolk." Parker held himself still, waiting for the bad news.

"That's about to change." The smug look was back on Norfolk's face. "If you want to see your Flemish painter alive, you'll start listening to me very, very closely."

———

Her satchel sat abandoned against the far wall of the Queen's antechamber. Parker lifted the bag up, because she would not forgive him if it was lost.

"Sir?"

Parker turned and saw a young woman he recognized from court. She was holding a piece of paper in her hands, and she stepped boldly from the huddle of women that had formed when he'd flung the door open and stormed in with the surprised yeomen at his heels.

"I see from the way you touch Mistress Horenbout's satchel that you care for her."

She looked at him intently, then flicked her eyes toward the door.

"You are right." Parker held out his arm as naturally as he could.

She took it with a smile and a curtsy.

"I do not know who arranged for her abduction, sir." The woman pitched her voice for his ears alone. "It could be one of the ladies, although I did see a servant look overlong at her when they came to deliver the Queen's repast to her chamber."

Parker felt a jolt at that. Norfolk had made use of servants throughout his scheme. But to have someone serving the Queen . . . The thought lodged sharp-edged shards of ice in his gut.

"That alone is valuable information. Thank you." They were nearing the door, although Parker was walking as slowly as he could.

She spoke quickly. "I saw the woman she spoke with. I think the woman who lured Mistress Horenbout out of the room is Norfolk's mistress. My mother knows his wife, who has complained about the woman many times. She once pointed her out to my mother, although they were not aware I was listening to their conversation."

They had reached the door, and Parker bowed smartly over her hand. "My thanks," he murmured, his heart pounding at hearing her revelation.

She curtsied in return, and Parker stepped into the passageway.

"Halt."

The strident voice of Lady Guildford cut across the room. For a moment, Parker considered ignoring her.

"Parker." Her voice was like a whip crack.

He turned, his teeth clenched, impatient to be away.

"The Queen wishes to speak with you, sir."

Parker forced himself to bow. His smile would have done credit to a death mask. Norfolk had given him an hour to see for himself that Susanna was gone, and he had never dealt well with the Queen.

No matter his personal regard for her intelligence and her courtesy, they were both very aware where his loyalties lay. And he knew it rankled her that he knew far more than she about her husband's business.

Lady Guildford raised an imperious eyebrow. Parker stepped back into the room with an inward shout of frustration and made his way to the door of the inner sanctum.

Who could disobey a summons from the Queen?

32

The Chiefe Conditions and Qualities in a Courtier: To have the vertues of the minde, as justice, manlinesse, wisdome, temperance, staideness, noble courage, sober-moode, etc.

Of the Chief Conditions and Qualityes in a Waytyng Gentylwoman: Not willinglie to give eare to suche as report ill of other women.

The gentle rock of the rowboat knocked Susanna's forehead against the rough wood support of the side seat with every ripple that hit the bow. Splinters poked through the sack that encased her, digging into her skin and adding to her misery at being bound and gagged, lying in the filthy, icy water at the bottom of the boat.

She was alone, and in this they had been especially wily. They had stuffed her into a hessian sack that stank of oily, wet wool and to the casual eye she was nothing but a lump at the bottom of a small, battered boat tied just off the banks of the river.

Parker would never think to look for her here.

Norfolk would be trying to extort something from him for

her safe return. Silence, or aid. And Parker might just accede to his demands to buy a little time to find her, even though he must know as well as she did that Norfolk would never let either of them live.

The icy puddle of water in the well of the boat had seeped through the sack, through her velvet dress, and dug cold fingers into her skin.

She shivered, and the toe of her slipper snagged on something. She tried to hold herself still and feel what it was.

The small opening at the neck of the sack.

She stretched her legs out and kicked, trying not to upset the boat. If it overturned she would sink to the bottom of the Thames. The drawstring stretched open a little way, and then the knot held.

Susanna wiggled her foot, testing for any weakness. The cord pulled tighter into an even more secure knot.

She gave in to frustration and panic, slamming her feet into the side of the small boat. It rocked wildly, tipping deeply to the left, and Susanna froze in terror. When at last the rocking subsided, she said a prayer of thanks.

She couldn't afford the luxury of panic. She thought of what Parker might be doing to save her. Thought of everything she had to lose, and then carefully pushed her foot into the opening again.

Y our Majesty." Parker bowed low, then he stood before her chair by the fire. She was sewing Henry's fine linen shirts, her plump, delicate fingers moving easily over the fabric.

"It is not like you to bring intrigue and danger to my chambers, Parker." She inclined her head toward a chair beside hers, and despite his wish to be off as soon as possible, Parker forced himself to sit without haste or hesitation.

"No, it isn't." He sat straight, ready to rise.

"You cannot tell me the details." It was not a question and she spoke stoically. There was a time, before Parker had come to court, when the Queen would have known the details all too well. Would have been advising Henry. When Katherine's father made an alliance with the Emperor behind Henry's back, her husband had never trusted her counsel again.

The Queen took his long silence for agreement and sighed. "What *can* you tell me, Parker?"

"That time is of the essence. Every minute I lose could be disastrous."

"It is even less like you to be melodramatic." She looked at him with clear eyes, and Parker could not help but wonder if she was comparing him to Henry, who loved melodrama. "So I can only assume you are speaking true."

Parker waited for her to dismiss him, but she stretched the moment out longer.

He must have made some movement, a twitch of impatience, because she smiled. There was something petulant in the quirk of her lips.

"I'm sorry. I should not tease you, but it is all the power I have these days. I give you leave to go."

Parker stood and bowed again, forcing himself to keep his

eyes on her, to give her the respect of her station. "My thanks, Your Majesty."

She waved him off, but as he bowed, he saw her expression briefly turn bitter.

He couldn't blame her.

33

The Chiefe Conditions and Qualities in a Courtier:
Not to folowe his own fansie, or alter the expresse
wordes in any point of his commission from hys
Prince or Lorde, onlesse he be assured that the
profit will be more, in case it have good successe,
then the damage, if it succeade yll.

*Of the Chief Conditions and Qualityes in a Waytyng
Gentylwoman:* To devise sportes and pastimes.

Two men stood near Norfolk's rooms. They looked up, tense, as Parker strode forward, and he noted they were roughly dressed.

They moved to stand shoulder to shoulder, blocking the way to the door, but Parker didn't slow down and he had no weapon in either hand. He sensed their surprise, their confusion as he came within striking distance.

"Halt." One man lifted a thick stick as he spoke, and Parker smiled at him and kept coming. The man jerked back a half-step, a moment before Parker leaped and punched him in the face. In the same movement, he lifted his left arm up and across, slamming his elbow into the second man's ear. As both fell, Parker flicked his arm, and straightened with his knife in hand. The two lay stunned and groaning on the floor.

It didn't begin to ease his anger at Susanna's taking. His hand clenched tight around the knife hilt as he struggled with the yearning to draw blood.

"If you are still in the palace by the time I call the Yeomen of the Guard, you'll go to the Tower. I would think you have less than a half hour." He spoke with quiet conviction, and the men dragged themselves to their feet and staggered away.

Parker took out the key he had requested from the Keeper of Greenwich Palace and turned it in the lock.

Norfolk stood beside his desk, and Parker could tell from the dart of his eyes that he knew Parker had overcome his guards. He swallowed convulsively. "There are plenty more where those came from."

Parker slammed the door behind him. "Given the rank amateurs you've drafted into this, I'm sure you're right." He lifted his knife. "Where is she, you bastard?"

Norfolk did not hide his satisfaction. "My rank amateurs did a creditable job of spiriting her away, don't you think?" He smiled and lifted a goblet from the table, then took a sip of wine. "Keeping servants in my employ has never proved so beneficial as today. I thought your little painter would be behind a locked door, so imagine my delight to discover she was in the Queen's chamber. And who among us can turn down a direct summons from the Queen?"

Parker readjusted his grip on his knife handle.

"Tsk, tsk, Parker." Norfolk laughed. "Given that her life

hangs in the balance, it's in your interest to keep me alive and well."

Parker fought the rage and the panic and the fear behind a blank mask, and his body shuddered as he pinned it under control.

"What do you want?"

"That must surely be obvious. I want you to become blind, deaf, and dumb, Parker. I want you to say nothing as I bring forward startling, worrying intelligence that the King's most trusted men are betraying him." Norfolk stroked the gold chain around his neck.

"When do you plan to do it?"

"This evening, just before dinner."

"And what happens if I say nothing?"

Norfolk lifted an eyebrow. "*If* you say nothing, when you return from the furor, you will find her back in her chamber."

"What is to stop me speaking out when I have her back?"

Norfolk shrugged. "The damage would be done. The seed planted. That's all I need."

"How can I trust you?" Parker's knuckles tightened to white as he gripped his blade.

Norfolk crossed his arms over his chest. "The only certainty is that if you cross me, she *will* die."

Parker watched him for a long moment, then turned and swung the door open.

"See you in the dining hall, Parker." Norfolk's call was soft.

Parker's footsteps didn't falter. The coldness in Norfolk's eyes set every instinct humming. No matter how he played this, the only way he'd see Susanna again was if he found her himself.

And he had less than three hours to do it.

———————

Anything?" Parker detached himself from the deep shadow of the courtyard wall as Harry came out of the kitchens, munching on an apple.

Harry nodded, and Parker went back to his dark alcove, making space for Harry to join him.

"Nothing on the Queen's servant—no one knows, or they ain't talking, if someone there is taking bribes from Norfolk. But they were talking about a man who bribed a few of them to keep off that back staircase for fifteen minutes during the midday repast."

Harry stopped to swallow and Parker grabbed the apple out of his hand. "We've got three hours before Norfolk kills her, so talk."

"The man was abrasive and high-handed, insulted most of them even as he paid them. One of 'em thought he was Norfolk's groom, and then another servant said he'd heard Norfolk was trying to get his mistress into the Queen's apartments, see if the Queen would take her as a maid of honor. That way he could have her at court at the King's expense."

Norfolk's mistress. The jolt of shock he'd felt when the maid of honor had said the same thing slammed into him again. It was the least cautious move Norfolk had made. A man's mistress was a direct link to him, the first time Norfolk

had allowed his own hand to be seen so close to the action.
The act of a desperate man.

"I want to find that mistress. But first, the groom." He slid
a knife off his belt, the one he'd taken from Fielder the day
before, and handed it to Harry.

"A loan?" Harry's eyes widened.

"It's yours. Let's go find Susanna."

Harry touched the knife with something approaching rever-
ence, and Parker recalled the day his own father had given him
a small bow to practice with. A rite of passage. He waited until
Harry had attached the sheath to his belt, then stepped out of
cover to make for the stables. Harry flanked him on his right.

The three men huddled for warmth around a small fire just
outside the stable door were friends of Simon's. Parker stepped
up to them easily.

"I have a problem." He kept his voice pitched low.

They stepped closer, heads bent toward him.

"I need to find Norfolk's groom, and I need to find him
before he knows I'm looking for him."

There was a moment of silence.

"What's he done?" The cartman who asked had worked
under Simon more than once, and Parker knew he was steady.
He saw him taking stock of Harry before returning his gaze to
Parker.

"Betrayed the King." No reason to make it more compli-
cated than that. There was no motivation stronger than helping to find a traitor. Accomplices tended to come to just as
bad an end as the main villain.

"Far stall, with some fancy light-skirt." The cartman jerked his head in the direction of the massive barn.

Could Norfolk's groom be keeping Susanna in the far stall, under the pretense he was entertaining a whore? Parker was gripped by the quick, heady flutter of hope, the thrill of anticipation, the yearning once more to draw blood.

He drew his sword and his knife, and all three men stepped back.

"Reckon you need help?" The young groom who spoke had the fire of action in his eyes. He took a step closer to Harry, as if to join them.

Parker gave a brief nod of acknowledgment. "Can you each take an entrance? Make sure no one enters or leaves?"

"Sir." The cartman touched his forehead.

Parker stepped into the stable, Harry behind him like a shadow, and moved forward silently on the hard earth floor to the end of the first row of stalls, then cut across to the far back.

There was silence in the last stall, and he was about to approach it when someone spoke. Parker crouched down. He looked back to make sure Harry had done the same, and crept forward.

"You sure she can breathe in that sack?"

It was a woman, but not Susanna, and the crush of disappointment hit Parker like a body blow. He forced himself to concentrate.

"Maybe not well, but enough to keep her alive. That's all she has to be, alive." A man's voice, low, with an edge of impatience.

"I hope you're right. Norfolk may need to use her later."

There was a nasty chuckle. "As long as she's breathing, that's all he needs. The more subdued she is, the better."

The silence stretched out, so long that Parker readied himself to leap in.

Someone shifted in the hay. "We better hope this goes to plan," the woman said.

"Aye. That is certainly my hope." The man's voice seemed level, but there was a timbre to it. Greed.

"You going to check on the boat?"

"In a bit. Don't want to draw attention to it. It's tied upstream, close to the palace." There was a rustle, as if he was making himself more comfortable.

Parker raised both blades and swung into the stall. He wanted to skewer them both, but he needed answers first. "I'll check that boat for you. Tell me where it is."

34

The Chiefe Conditions and Qualities in a Courtier: To be an honest, a faire condicioned man, and of an upright conscience.

Of the Chief Conditions and Qualityes in a Waytyng Gentylwoman: To be of good condicions and well brought up.

The shock on their faces should have been sweet, but all Parker could think of was who would be the most likely to talk. They lay side by side in the hay, completely at his mercy.

He chose the groom. He was the servant who'd approached Norfolk in the garden earlier, and Parker recognized him as an opportunist. Greed was predictable. He wasn't sure what Norfolk's mistress's motivation was. The tip of his sword prodded the man's throat, but he kept his knife ready and pointed in the woman's direction. Harry was out of sight by the door to the stall, watching his back.

"Well? Where upstream is this boat tied?" Parker pressed the sword at an angle, and opened a thin cut on the stretched skin of the groom's throat.

The man swallowed, his Adam's apple working, but he said nothing.

Parker leaned harder.

"Wait." The groom swallowed again, and shot a quick look at the woman. "What do I get out of it?"

Parker narrowed his eyes. "I'll give you a ten-minute head start to run for your life."

The groom closed his eyes, tried to find some peace in failure. Parker saw the moment he accepted it. "The boat is—"

"No! You can't betray him!" the woman shrieked, and lunged. Parker saw the knife in her hand too late and moved to parry, but it was not aimed at him.

She slashed it across her companion's throat, the sharp blade opening him like a gutted fish.

The groom convulsed, fighting for air, the blood pulsing out of him in ever-weakening beats.

Norfolk's mistress turned eyes on him that made Parker step back. Pale blue, ice cold, their intensity was exaggerated by the thin ribbons of blood latticed across her face.

"Go to hell," she said, her voice detached, emotionless. She looked down and saw she was sitting in a widening pool of blood. Her hand opened and the knife fell into the hay. She began to rock, her disconcerting gaze never leaving Parker's face.

"Harry, don't come in here. Call the cartman."

Parker took a firm grip on his sword and crouched down, flicking her knife to the far side of the stall.

The woman was unbalanced, beyond reason. Was she as

important to Norfolk as Susanna was to him? He'd find out soon enough, but he'd only try to exchange one woman for the other as a last resort. Norfolk wouldn't like the turnabout, and Parker wasn't prepared to risk Susanna's life on the gamble that Norfolk cared deeply for his mistress.

He heard the cartman and the two grooms behind him, heard their gasps of shock. He straightened up, eager to be away. The clock was ticking, and while the fate of a realm hung in the balance, the only thing he cared about now was getting Susanna back.

"Watch her. And get her knife." Parker lifted his own clean weapons to show them he'd had nothing to do with the carnage. "Find a place to tuck her away until I can deal with her. And tie her up."

"God's teeth." The cartman edged into the stall and picked the knife up gingerly by the hilt. "We'll see to it."

"My thanks." Parker turned and saw Harry standing in the doorway, his eyes wide. "I told you not to come in. There are some things you can never unsee."

Harry stepped out and leaned weakly against the wall. "I was curious." He looked close to vomiting.

"Pull yourself together." Parker saw the cartman frown at his coldness, but he had no time for niceties, and a purpose would focus Harry's mind away from the gruesome sight. There truly *was* no time to indulge in shock. "We have a boat to find, on a river full of boats."

Was that someone calling her name?

Susanna tried to still the shivering in her body. The chatter of her teeth and the shaking made it difficult to hear.

The call sounded again, faint but coming closer. Was that Harry?

Her throat was raw from screaming, but she did it again, shouting into her gag. All it produced was a muffled groan.

Still, her heart pounded with renewed energy. If they knew to look on the river, perhaps they knew she was in a boat. She needed to make the boat stand out from the others, make it draw the eye.

She raised her legs, wondering if her sack-covered feet lifted high enough to be seen over the gunwales of the boat. The boat rocked slightly as she made the movement, and an idea formed.

Terror and hope shook her more than the cold.

She began to rock the boat, centering herself as much as possible. Her tied arms cramped beneath her, and the momentum made her tip dangerously one way, then the other.

She rocked hard left, then right, until she was lifting up partway with each dip, slamming down and lifting again.

She hadn't heard Harry again. Suddenly panicked, she hammered her feet down with each rolling rock. She fought the dark and the confinement. Fought the boat and the helplessness. Raged and rocked and arched her back. Fear wrapped chilly tentacles around her spine as the boat tipped past its axis.

She had fought too well.

The boat teetered until gravity exacted its price and she fell heavily downward.

She tried to pitch herself the other way, but she rolled like a bolster, felt the sharp, cold resistance of the rush of water into the boat, and then tumbled into the river.

As she went under, she heard a dull thud above her. The boat capsizing on the surface, slamming the lid on her coffin.

35

The Chiefe Conditions and Qualities in a Courtier:
Not to waite upon or serve a wycked and naughtye
person.

*Of the Chief Conditions and Qualityes in a Waytyng
Gentylwoman:* To flee affectation or curiositie.

P arker reached the end of a cluster of boats as the daylight
faded. Dusk was closing in, leaching the sun away ray by
precious ray. In an hour or less it would be dark.

He was panting as if he'd run ten miles, panic clawing at
his insides. Norfolk's man had said upstream from the palace,
and he was standing by the last clutch of upstream vessels
before the rough dock gave way to a small field.

"Susanna!" His shout made the bargemen turn to him. The
rowboats beside him bumped and ground together as the tide
rose.

Where is she?

Downstream of where he stood, nearer Harry than himself,
an old rowboat began rocking wildly. Too wildly for it to be

the work of the tide. He took a step closer, and it tipped deeply to the left.

A brown hessian sack splashed into the water and sank out of sight, and the boat flipped upside down on top of it.

Parker hurtled down the quay, a sob in his throat, ripping his belt, his cloak, his doublet off as he ran. He was at the end, legs bracing to leap off, when the sack lifted up from the water, gave a little hop, and fell back under.

Parker jumped, his feet sinking into the sludge, the water thigh-high. He reached below the murky surface and hauled Susanna up.

"Here." Harry was there too, holding out Fielder's knife.

"Stay still, Susanna." Parker took the knife from Harry and carefully sliced the sack open.

Her cool forest eyes looked back at him out of a face speckled with mud and grime. Her mouth was gagged, her forehead bruised.

It was the most beautiful sight he had ever seen.

———

He had found her. Susanna stood in his arms and marveled that she could stand at all. Could breathe, hold, and love.

He kissed her forehead gently and drew her closer before setting her away. "I'm sorry, love. It isn't over yet."

As he spoke, the long, mournful cry of a bugle sounded, and then another. The King was returned from the hunt.

"We need to dress and get to the great hall before Norfolk begins his mischief."

Susanna clutched at him, grabbing fistfuls of wet linen shirt in her hands. "Wait." Her hands were clenched so tight with cold and desperation, she wondered if she'd be able to let go. "Parker." She tried to read his face, but his mask had come down the moment the bugle sounded, and she would have to take a chance.

He held himself still, his full focus on her. She lifted on her toes and brushed her cold lips over his. "I am yours."

His mask fell away, and she felt the full force of his heat. His searing, engulfing heat. "And I am yours." He took her hands, and pried them gently from his shirt. "Let's go get the bastard."

Norfolk had almost reached the King's side. He was only steps away from where Henry sat on a low dais. Parker began to plow through the crowd, rage and dread giving his elbows extra force.

Susanna clung to his doublet as she followed. He glanced back to check on her. He would not let her out of his sight again.

"Parker!"

Someone shoved through the crush and grabbed his arm, stopping Parker dead. Relief whipped through him when he realized it was Simon.

"What news?" He had no hopes it would be good. "Did you find Pettigrew?"

"No." Simon swayed from side to side and his eyes blazed excitement in a face haggard with fatigue. "I went straight to the docks to look for him—but there I met a messenger just off a boat from France and received the most unbelievable news. I didn't even look for Pettigrew. I turned around and rode back to London without stopping; haven't slept since I left you."

Parker felt the first stirrings of hope, and let Simon pull them away from the crowd to one side of the room.

"De la Pole is dead. Killed in battle at Pavia." Simon's hands shook, and he rubbed them over his face. "And more, the King of France is captured."

Satisfaction crashed through Parker, making it hard to breathe. "Then Norfolk is hanging in the breeze. There is no army from France to back him."

His eyes went to the dais where Norfolk now stood with the King.

Their eyes met.

Norfolk's gaze jerked from him, widening at the sight of Susanna and Simon standing with him. Parker sent him a vicious smile.

Sweat, you bastard. Feel the fear.

He turned back to Simon, motioned him toward the King.

Simon shook his head. "'Tis your news to give, Parker. I would not have been in Dover if not for you, and you have paid the highest price in this."

Parker frowned. "There will surely be a boon for this information."

"And you deserve it. Imagine what you could ask of the King." Simon bowed very deliberately to Susanna, and Parker saw her frown and look between them.

"Then come with me. Let us bring Norfolk down together."

"I have no argument with that."

Parker took Susanna's arm, and Simon flanked her other side. Together they approached the dais.

Norfolk watched them with the interest of a fox watching the hounds, and as they came toward him he took a quick step forward to block them from the King. "I have something urgent to tell you, Your Majesty." He sounded out of breath.

"I'm sure whatever it is, it can wait for news from Dover." Parker put a foot up on the low stage. "The King will wish to hear this."

Suddenly unsure, Norfolk took a deep step back. Parker smiled.

"Well?" Henry asked.

"De la Pole is dead." Parker bowed. "And the King of France is captured."

Norfolk lost all color, and Henry sprang to his feet, his mouth agape.

"Dead? Captured?" The King seemed unsure whether to believe it.

"At a battle at Pavia, Your Majesty."

"Ale. Ale for all. Ale for everyone in London!" The King laughed out loud. "All the enemies of England are gone."

Parker held Norfolk's stricken gaze.

Not all of them.

———

"This is most excellent news." Norfolk's voice was high and thin, and he cleared his throat. "Parker, I must speak with you."

There was something sly and furtive in his sidelong look that sent a light touch of dread down Parker's spine.

"What is this? You must celebrate. This is no time for work, gentlemen." Henry clapped his hands. "Music. Merry music!"

Norfolk stepped down from the dais and bent his head close to Parker's. "You'll want to hear what I have to say."

Parker exchanged a quick look with Susanna, then with Simon. Simon shrugged.

Silently, they followed Norfolk to the back of the great hall and into a small chamber to one side. Simon closed the door behind them.

"I'm sure nothing gives you greater pleasure than my current difficulty, Parker. But if I go down, I refuse to go down alone."

"I don't care who you bring down with you, Norfolk. Anyone in league with you deserves what they get." Parker reached for the door handle.

"Wait. Listen. Buckingham's execution a few years ago shook the nobility in this country. He was foolish to move his troops around, foolish to talk so arrogantly about his eligibility for the throne, but no one believed the King would have had him executed were it not for Wolsey."

Norfolk wet his lips. "I've had a King's Groom of the Body in my pay for some years, and I made sure he knew to check the fireplace for letters that might have been thrown there. And one day he brought me one that was hardly singed by the flames. Carelessly written, and carelessly discarded."

With a deliberate tug, Norfolk set a sleeve right. "A letter from the King to Wolsey, refusing to grant Buckingham clemency. Wolsey was begging him to spare Buckingham. The King would not be swayed." He straightened the other sleeve, as if the exact line mattered a great deal. "He had the good sense to think better of sending it. And all this time everyone thought Wolsey brought Buckingham low, not the King. But it *was* him."

"What does that matter?" Susanna asked. "He's the King; he can have a traitor executed. It's his right."

"But a very unpopular move. And not one that should have been entered into lightly." Simon crossed his hands over his chest.

"The tone of the letter, the arrogance and the flippancy of it . . ." Norfolk's smile was sly. "It will cause a great deal of unhappiness—at a time when there is no male heir to the throne. Just one little girl and an illegitimate boy."

Parker clenched his fists, closed his eyes. His plans to crush Norfolk were crumbling to dust in front of him.

"What is he saying?" Susanna put a hand on his arm.

Parker had to force the words out of his mouth. "He's saying that unless we keep silent about his involvement with de la Pole, he has the means to bring the country to war."

36

The Chiefe Conditions and Qualities in a Courtier: Sil-dome or never to sue to hys Lorde for anye thing for himself.

Of the Chief Conditions and Qualities in a Waytyng Gentylwoman: To showe suche a one all signes and tokens of love savynge suche as maye put hym in anye dyshonest hope.

B efore she left the celebration, Susanna caught his eye and smiled. The kind of smile that made him think of a dark room and a comfortable bed.

"I seek leave to go, Your Majesty." Parker tried to slip from the King's hold around his neck.

"Go? No, no, Parker. You must celebrate." Henry's words were beginning to slur.

He wanted to celebrate, all right. But not with the King.

As Susanna slipped from the room, at the sight of her narrow back, the flick of her velvet skirt, he turned to Henry. "I have a boon to ask."

"A boon?" Henry struggled to his feet, hauling Parker up

with him. "Parker would have a boon of me!" The King's shout echoed around the room.

Parker held himself still. He should have known better than to ask now.

There were yells and boos and cheers from the crowd.

"What would you have of me, my friend? My bearer of good news?"

Parker looked at the now-quieter gathering of courtiers, saw the avid curiosity in their faces. What the hell. At least he could extract this promise with witnesses. There would be no going back for Henry if it didn't suit him when he was sober.

"I would have permission to take a wife."

The roar of approval deafened him, swelling around the room and crashing over him like a tidal wave.

"Parker the Cold? Parker the Merciless? Parker the Lone Wolf? Would take a wife?" Henry tugged Parker even closer in the headlock. "Is she wealthy or connected to the nobility?"

"No."

There was laughter again; some of it closer to sniggers.

"But then why do you want her?" Henry's voice was quiet, which forced the others to quieten as well.

Parker studied those in the room, saw some friends, even more enemies, and did not care who heard. "I would marry for love, Your Majesty."

Henry released him, stood back, and watched Parker closely. "For love? Ah. What a thing. What a privilege." He turned away, and Parker thought it in dismissal, felt cold dread at what such a reaction would mean. Henry turned back, a finger brushing a tear from his eye as he composed himself. "Then so you shall."

Parker bowed deeper, lower than he had ever bowed before. "My thanks, Your Majesty." He was across the room and at the door before anyone had the idea to drink to his happiness.

The Yeomen of the Guard let him through with smirks, and the door closed behind him.

Susanna stood, hands gathered at her breast, in the deep gloom of the passage.

"Did you hear everything?" His voice was not his own.

"Some of it. The roar of the crowd brought me back. I was afraid something was wrong."

"You may think it presumptuous that I asked the King's permission first, but I could not ask you without knowing I had leave to do so." He tried to read her eyes, but they were shadowed.

"And if he had refused?" She stepped closer, and still he could not read her. His usually open Susanna.

"If he had refused, I would still have asked you."

"And if I had said yes?"

"Then we would be packing our things and finding the next ship to Ghent."

She smiled, slowly and from the heart out.

"I still say yes."

He lifted a finger to her cheek. "And we have no need to pack at all." He looked at her and saw everything. A lifetime. A wonderful adventure. "Let's get to our chamber."

She lifted an eyebrow. "Parker the Cold?"

"Not that cold." He let her see the heat in his gaze.

"Parker the Merciless?"

He took her arm in polite courtesy and bared his teeth. "You will see how merciless I can be."

"Parker the Lone Wolf?"

He lifted her fingers to his lips. "Not so lonely anymore."

AUTHOR'S NOTE

This is a work of fiction, although where possible I have tried to stay true to what happened during this exciting time in England's history. John Parker really was the Keeper of the Palace of Westminster and Henry's Yeoman of the Crossbows, although he was later promoted to Keeper of the King's Robes. I couldn't find out when this change occurred, and crossbows are so much more interesting than robes, so Parker is yet to be promoted in my telling of the tale.

Susanna Horenbout is even more difficult to pin down. She really was praised by Albrecht Dürer, and he really did buy her work when she was just eighteen. On her death, she was further praised by eminent Renaissance artists, but no known work of hers survives. My thanks go to art historians Lorne Campbell and Susan Foister for their in-depth study of the life of Susanna and her father and brother. I drew heavily from their research to flesh out Susanna's history.

I don't know the circumstances of Parker and Susanna's meeting, courtship, and marriage, but it is quite true that they did marry.

Of the complete fabrications, I concocted the plot by de la

Pole to get papal backing for his claim to the throne of England, but I did not make up the secret treaty between the King of France and the Pope. It got me thinking that if such a treaty was in effect, de la Pole might have tried to use it for his own ends, and I took things from there.

I also made up Norfolk's plot to overthrow the crown. He did hate Cardinal Wolsey, and his father did cry as he sentenced Buckingham to the chopping block for treason. Most believed Wolsey was behind Buckingham's execution, but today we know that it was in fact on Henry's insistence.

I fabricated entirely Henry's obsession with Cesare Borgia. I have no idea whether he admired the man or not; but given Henry's love for knightly honor and courage on the battlefield, I thought Borgia might have been a hero he would have believed in. And Borgia did conveniently (for my purposes) die around the time Henry was mysteriously locked away by his father. No one seems to know why Henry VII secluded Henry VIII in that way, so I devised a reason.

Also, while George Boleyn was a womanizer and most probably a rapist (he confessed to living a depraved life before he was executed, although he denied the accusations of incest with his sister), and while he did visit his infamous sister Anne at the court of Margaret of Austria, I have no idea if he was sent away from there in disgrace. It could have happened, given his abhorrent behavior, and as this is a work of fiction, I made it so.

Francis Bryan did throw stones and eggs at people in the streets of Paris with the French King; back home, he affected

French manners at court and spoke scornfully of English manners and dress. He was a consummate courtier, playing the game any way he could to ingratiate himself with the King. His sister Elizabeth, who married his friend Nicholas Carew, was most likely one of Henry's mistresses.

So much of my knowledge of King Henry VIII and his court comes from the reference works of Alison Weir. I thank the stars for a historian like her. Her work is both encyclopedic in its detail and incredibly accessible.

IN A
TREACHEROUS
COURT

MICHELLE DIENER

INTRODUCTION

While en route to England from the Netherlands, royally commissioned artist Susanna Horenbout discovers a secret that could jeopardize the reign of King Henry VIII. As she and John Parker, one of the monarch's most enigmatic courtiers, evade the ruthless enemy seeking to silence her, they become entwined in a deadly plot that reaches to the upper echelons of the royal inner circle. In *In a Treacherous Court*, Michelle Diener brings two of Tudor England's most fascinating, lesser-known historical figures vividly to life in a dazzling tale of intrigue and romance.

TOPICS AND QUESTIONS FOR DISCUSSION

1. As an artist commissioned by King Henry VIII, Susanna journeys to England for professional reasons. Discuss the personal circumstances that also compel her to leave Ghent. Why does she feel she has been "exiled" from her home?

2. The story takes place over a period of several days, during which Susanna and Parker go from just meeting each other to becoming engaged. How did you react to this rapid progression? Why do they trust each other implicitly almost from the start?

3. Susanna and Parker both have unusual backgrounds that set them apart from conventional society—as a female artist, she is a rarity, while he comes from an upper-class family but ended up in poverty. In what ways do these experiences influence their personal connection?

4. "She was trouble. He'd heard of these women in the Netherlands and Italy, whose fathers took them into their studios and trained them in the arts of painting and sculpture along with their brothers," (p. 6) notes Parker when he first meets Susanna. Discuss how women artists are perceived in this society. Why do you think Susanna's father choose this life for her? What kind of say did Susanna have in this decision?

5. Susanna admits that her training as an artist is "a mixed blessing" (p. 35). In what ways is it a benefit? How about a detriment? How do Susanna's artistic skills help them uncover the plot against the King?

6. "I would make a poor wife," (p. 100) Susanna tells Parker. Why does she believe that her career as an artist will prohibit her from marrying? Were you surprised when she later agreed to marry Parker?

7. Parker has a different relationship with Henry VIII than most, if not all, of the King's other courtiers. Why does he feel such a deep sense of loyalty to the King? In what ways

is Parker different from the typical aristocrats at court? How do his fellow courtiers view him?

8. After Parker discovers that the Duke of Norfolk is behind the plot to overthrow Henry VIII, how does he turn the tables on the nobleman? In what ways does Susanna play a crucial role in their pursuit to protect the throne? How are both of their fates intertwined with that of the King?

9. Discuss the scene on page 251 when Susanna joins the Queen's ladies-in-waiting. What does it reveal about the roles of women in courtly life? How do the ladies' reactions to Susanna's artistic talent differ from those of the men she has encountered?

10. What prompts the normally reserved Parker to do something so out of character and ask the King for permission to marry Susanna in front of a gathering of courtiers? What do you think he would have done if the King had refused his request?

11. In the Author's Note, Michelle Diener explains which aspects of *In a Treacherous Court* were based on true events and which ones she created for the novel. Share your thoughts on the story line, including the romantic and mystery elements. What is your opinion of how the author presents more well-known historical figures, like Henry VIII and George Boleyn?

12. How does *In a Treacherous Court* compare to other works of historical fiction your group has read, including books set in Tudor England? Are you interested in reading Michelle Diener's follow-up novel to *In a Treacherous Court*? Why or why not?

ENHANCE YOUR BOOK CLUB

1. As a nod to Susanna's profession, take an art class, visit a gallery or museum, or provide supplies and have members try their hands at sketching before your discussion of *In a Treacherous Court*.

2. In the Author's Note, Michelle Diener praises Alison Weir and "thank[s] the stars for a historian like her." Along with *In a Treacherous Court*, read and discuss Weir's nonfiction work *Henry VIII: The King and His Court*.

3. Set a festive scene for your book club discussion by hosting a "royal" get-together. Ideas for food, décor, and more can be found at www.ehow.com/way_5155294_royal-theme-party-decoration-ideas.html.